STRONG ALIBI

ELIZABETH STRONG MYSTERY BOOK 2

K.C. TURNER

E.M. HANDLY

TWO TEN PRESS

STRONG ALIBI
Elizabeth Strong Mystery Book 2
Second Edition

E.M. Handly
writing as
K.C. Turner

Published by Two Ten Press
Reprinted with author permission.

eBook ISBN: 978-1-7367415-2-8
Print ISBN: 978-1-7367415-3-5

TRIGGER WARNINGS

The Elizabeth Strong Mystery Series deals with topics that may be sensitive or triggering for some readers, including but not limited to domestic violence, sexual assault, abuse and other criminal activity.

If you or someone you know needs support, please reach out for help. If you have an emergency, do not hesitate to call 911.

National Domestic Violence Hotline
800-799-7233
National Sexual Assault Hotline
800-656-4673
National Hotline for Mental Health and Suicide Prevention
800-273-TALK (8255)

CHAPTER 1

The rain pelted the leaves as her bare feet bore into the earth, forming puddles in their wake with each stride she took. She stopped and hid behind the biggest tree in sight to try and gain her composure. The storm nearly drowned out the sound of his voice.

"Liz-zy..."

Her head spun in his direction, flipping a lock of drenched blonde hair over her eye to rest against her tiny nose. She stood silent, motionless. Looking ahead, she could make out the porch light above Marta's door in the distance. She closed her eyes for a moment and took a deep breath before propelling herself forward to run for safety, the mud oozing between her toes with each step.

"Lizzy!"

Running faster, the door handle was within her reach. Lunging for it, she quickly stopped before reaching the edge of the boat dock and waving her arms by her sides to catch her balance. The sound of his boots echoed with the thunder above them. She slowly turned around, succumbing to the weakness in her legs and fell to her knees before him. Her tears danced with the raindrops down her cheeks.

He moved closer to her, gradually raising the gun to her face. "I told you I would see you soon, Lizzy."

"Please!" she begged between breaths. The sound of the bullet leaving the barrel mixed poetically with her scream.

Thrashing the blankets as she woke, Elizabeth fell off the side of the bed, hitting her head against the night-stand. It hadn't affected her. She ripped off her sleep mask and placed her hands beside herself on the floor, taking large breaths in an attempt to pace the rapid heartbeats. She jumped up, ran to the bathroom, and fumbled in the cabinet for the bottle of Valium. After popping a pill into her mouth, she turned on the faucet and cupped her hands under the cold running water before taking a gulp and splashing her face with the remainder. Her reflection in the mirror was as pale as her hair. *When is this going to end?*

Before she could answer her own thoughts she heard the screen door open, the sound of clogs on the wooden porch floor, then loud knocking on the door to the dining room.

"Hello! Wakey, wakey, eggs and bakey!"

Elizabeth looked at herself one last time in the mirror,

smiled, and grabbed a face towel from the rack on the wall to her left. She walked past the table that seated six and un-bolted the door.

"Good morning, sunshine," exclaimed China as she breezed past Elizabeth and threw her beach bag on the table, just missing the fruit bowl.

Taking a deep breath, Elizabeth shut the door behind her friend and walked around the table to follow China into the kitchen.

"What the hell, Liz? No coffee? Did you forget I was coming over?" China finally turned around and actually looked at Elizabeth. Her slanted eyes grew wide with concern. "Honey! Are you okay?"

Leaning on the doorframe she replied, "I didn't forget. Sorry, I over slept and it wasn't as pleasant as it should have been." She raised her hand to stop China from hugging her. "Don't worry, I took a Valium."

China had learned when it was necessary to play counselor and when to leave well enough alone. "Well alright then," she said as she turned away and reached in the cabinet for the coffee. "Go get ready. By then we should have some liquid fuel ready to consume and the sun should be *per*-fect."

Elizabeth shut the door to the bathroom behind her and stripped out of her pajamas. She grabbed her coral colored, string bikini hanging from the doorknob and put it on her petite frame. She was always tiny, but the past three months had allowed her to gain a few pounds while remaining a size two, filling in her swimsuit quite nicely. A nice man in her life tends to do that to a woman. She brushed out her long blonde hair, put some tinted chap stick on her lips, and threw her sunscreen in her bag.

Meeting China back in the kitchen they grabbed the cooler, CD player, and to-go coffee cups before heading out the back door and down the trail to Marta's private beach. For as long as they had been friends, China rarely visited Elizabeth's home. It was typically the other way around. However, now that Elizabeth had the lake house and access to a boat and private beach, it didn't make much sense to go to China's. Sitting by a quiet lake and basking in the sun was much more relaxing than a hot tub surrounded by woods, depending on the season, of course.

Marta was Elizabeth's closest neighbor. She was also like a second mother. She and her husband Bill were close friends of the family for years and they took care of the lake house for Elizabeth after her parent's death and prior to her decision to move back. The lake house didn't have access to the beach but it had a private boat dock and a beautiful view. A wooded trail connected the two homes and Elizabeth had permission to use their beach whenever she liked.

Choosing a spot close to the water, they laid the sheet down, securing it from the breeze with the cooler and CD player. China lifted her white sarong over her head revealing her gleaming olive-toned skin. "This is so much better than a hot tub in 90 degree heat. I am so glad you moved here, Liz!"

Elizabeth made herself cozy on the sheet, digging her belly into the sand below and swept her hair over one shoulder. "I wish every day could be Saturday."

"So, tell me, why did you have such a bad night? You never sleep that late, especially if it's our beach day."

Taking a deep breath, Elizabeth confessed, "I had nightmares all night. It was bad. It was really bad."

"I knew it! Damn it, Liz, I thought you were going to the doctor to talk about this?"

"I did! She filled my script and told me I need to seriously consider going to the parole hearing."

Rolling onto her backside and leaning on her forearms, China glared at Elizabeth and said, "No kidding? That's what I've been telling you for months. You know, you could pay me privately and I'll be your personal shrink. Win, win!" She leaned her head back, shook her bangs out of her eyes and closed them to shut out the sun's rays.

"When you can give me my happy pills, I would be happy to be your life-long patient."

"I thought Martinez was coming over last night, anyway? Haven't you tapped into that Latin-love-fest yet?"

Flipping over onto her back, she sighed. "He ended up getting called out for a shooting. We barely made it past the first glass of wine. He's coming over tonight though.

Marta is having us over for dinner. You should stay and come with?"

"And be a third wheel? No thanks. Besides, I have a date already. Chester is taking me to a new place that just opened up in Cleveland."

Elizabeth couldn't help but laugh each time she heard it. The name didn't suit her friend's taste in men.

China rolled her eyes. "You know, you should be happy for me."

Laughing again, Elizabeth explained, "I am! I promise you I am. I'm glad you decided to give a guy a chance since John. And I'm even more glad you told Thomas to take a hike. You did tell Thomas to take a hike didn't you?"

China propelled her chin to the sky to even the coloring on her neck, remaining silent to the interrogation.

Elizabeth rolled back onto her belly and demanded, "Damn it, China! Please tell me you told him?"

Slinging her head to rest on her shoulder, she looked into Elizabeth's eyes. "I tried. It's complicated, okay? Give me a little time."

"A little time? That's all you've given him is time, while he plays house with the Blonde every night in their cozy, little ranch-style home."

"You're a fine one to talk. It's been three months and you haven't even skidded to second base with a guy who would bend over backwards for you. And what about that parole hearing? You have people backing you, Liz, and you refuse to take advantage."

"That's totally different!"

"Actually, it's not." China stood up and adjusted her bikini top. Her large, fake breasts barley covered. "I need to cool off," she said before stomping off and wading in the lake, careful not to wet her perfectly styled hair.

Elizabeth and China were more like sisters than they were best friends. They worked together, hung out together, and nearly shared everything; except their taste in men. *Treat me like shit and I'll follow you forever* seemed to be China's motto. Of course, Elizabeth didn't have the greatest track record either. Her ex-boyfriend was currently serving a prison sentence for nearly disfiguring her and he was up for parole in less than a week.

Sitting up and lacing her legs in a criss cross, Elizabeth reached into the cooler, pulling out a Corona and a pre-made sandwich. She popped the bottle cap with China's lighter and took a swig of her beer, staring out at the calm lake. China made her way back to their spot, sat heavily in the sand, and sighed.

Her mouth half full of ham and bread, Elizabeth turned to her and said, "I'm sorry."

Immediately turning to face her, China replied, "No you're not. But for what it's worth, I'm not sorry either." They looked at each other with mutual empathy and smiled. "Look, I know how you feel about the parole hearing, Liz, but you seriously need to reconsider this. This is a little different than what Thomas and I have going on, and on a whole other level than you and your Latin-lover. This is serious! What if he gets out? And what if the only thing that keeps him in is you showing up at that hearing and speaking your mind?"

"I'm not sure I can face him again, China."

She flicked her hair again. "You already did it once. Walk in the park."

"It's not just that. He's already proven he can get to me in or out of prison."

"Too bad your hero can't prove that. And frankly, I don't think he ever will. Johnnie Warren is part of a clan. Those guys never snitch on each other."

"Yeah, well, if he doesn't get out, he'll just find another goon to terrorize me. And if I have anything to do with keeping him *in*, when he *does* get out, he will hunt me down for sure."

China sighed as she rolled back onto her belly, leaning on her elbows, and flinging her manicured fingers in the air as she spoke. "Liz, I understand where you're coming from, I do. I thought Martinez was a good detective? He didn't get *anything* from Johnnie boy?"

"He's been trying for three months. He thought at one point he was going to waive his rights and roll on Steve but he refused to crack. For everything he put me through he gets a plea deal and probation. I guess Matthew Polk is a better attorney than we all thought."

Elizabeth thought for sure Johnnie Warren would go away for a while after stalking her, breaking into her house, and running her off the road. Of course, there wasn't enough evidence to prove some of the charges. And since she wasn't seriously injured in the car accident, not to mention the fact that he had a public defender who dreamed of being a big city defense attorney, Johnnie walked away with basically a slap on the hand. She didn't really care about him. She cared more about the man who truly wanted to hurt her, Steve Robinson. The man who everyone believed hired Johnnie to do his dirty work but no one could prove it. She could only hope his parole hearing went in her favor.

"Nope. Sorry, Polk is still an idiot. You would be a better attorney than he is. Johnnie just did what most people don't think of; he kept his mouth shut and took the deal offered to him. I just wish you would consider speaking at the hearing. You're the victim. You have every right to be there. Let him know he doesn't scare you anymore."

"Please stop saying that." She despised being referred to as a victim.

China rolled her eyes at the fact she had to be politically correct. "Excuse me. Sur-*vi*-vor. Come on, Liz."

"Maybe I am still a victim. Cheese and rice, I see a shrink every month; I take Valium like they're Tums; and yes, I admit it, he still scares the shit out of me. My showing up there is not going to sway the parole board's decision. We deal with victims every day. We're supposed to be their voice. How many times do you think the prosecutor and the judge really care what they think or what they have to say? If the defendant has a decent attorney and they accept a lesser charge, who cares? The prosecutors still get their win and the court still makes their money. Plain and simple."

"Well, I can't argue with that but we're not talking about the victims at work. We're talking about you. And I'm worried that psycho is going to get out. Can you just consider it? With Marilyn's recommendation and your face-to-face statement, there's probably a better chance of him *not* getting out."

Elizabeth took a deep breath. A part of her knew China was right. Marilyn Bennett was their boss. She was also Annapolis County's prosecuting attorney, who happened to prosecute the case against Steve and put him in Mansfield Correctional for eight years. Her written recommendation to keep him in would help, but it was still a mere recommendation and the parole board had no obligation to follow it.

It also didn't stop Elizabeth from thinking of the repercussions if she showed up to speak at the hearing. Steve was a manipulator. He was cunning and slick in his maneuvers. She was sure he already had a plan of attack. She was sure he had been planning it for the past six years while he was locked up.

Placing her empty bottle in the cooler and lying on her back to face the rays she said, "Look, I'll think about it. Can we just enjoy the rest of our beach day and talk about something else? Or, not talk about anything?"

China gave her a sigh. "Sorry, I won't say anything more about it."

Elizabeth looked at her pursing her lips as if she didn't believe her.

"Okay, okay! I promise. Not another word," she said as she dug her bum into the sand and laid her head down to rest.

They basked in the sun for hours in near silence as the sweat beads formed on top of their tanning lotion. A jet ski passed in the distance and tiny waves rolled upon the shoreline in its wake. Elizabeth rolled over, gently rubbed her eyes, and looked to her phone for the time. "Wow, it's almost two o'clock already. Are you about ready to head back?"

China moaned, "Do we have to? Just a little longer?"

"Okay, one more beer and then I would like to take a nap before dinner. Angel will be here around six."

"You should really stop calling him Angel. It sounds too, well, angelic. Mar-ti-nez…" she said with a roll of the tongue. "Just sounds sexier, ya know?"

Grinning, Elizabeth flirted, "Hmm. How do you know I don't?"

She was rather excited for her date and had the entire evening planned. Angel Martinez was the first man Elizabeth had even considered dating since her previous relationship ended in such a disaster. For six years she warded off men in general. So much so, all of the attorneys she encountered at court accused her of being a man hater. She didn't hate men: Quite the contrary. She simply hated men who beat their women.

As a court advocate for women of domestic violence,

defense attorneys were rarely looking for Elizabeth's opinion on anything. Not that she cared in the least what they thought of her. She fought them every step of the way when the situation and her victim called for it. Angel was different. Not only was he one of Silverton, Ohio's finest detectives, helping to put away the psychopaths of the world, he and Elizabeth were a lot alike on many levels. Most importantly, they were both survivors trying to fight the good fight.

Elizabeth lightly shook China's arm to wake her out of her sun coma. "China, hey, sorry hun, but we should get back."

Groaning and reluctantly moving from her bed in the sand, China said, "Noooo! Ugh, beach day can't be over."

"We still have a few good weeks left," she reassured.

They gathered their things after shaking out the sand and walked back to the lake house. Reaching her vehicle, China reached over to Elizabeth, hugged her tight, and grasped her shoulders before saying, "Have a great time tonight." She flung her beach bag into the back seat and asked, "What are you doing tomorrow? Wanna get together."

"I was kind of planning on brunch. In bed."

China shook her hips in a sexy manner. "Well I'll be damned! Lookin' to have a little sausage gravy on your biscuit, eh?" she said shaking her head up and down.

"Eew," exclaimed Elizabeth as she slapped China's arm. "I swear you are impossible. I promise I will fill you in first thing Monday morning."

Making her way into her vehicle, China looked to the sun and bellowed, "Soo-*ey!*" Then she laughed deep from her belly and yelled out her window as she backed out of the driveway, "You know I love you, Liz!"

Shaking her head, Elizabeth turned away with a smile on her face and swatted her hand in the air towards her friend before heading into the house for a much needed beauty rest.

CHAPTER 2

*M*artinez and Elizabeth stood at the front door to Marta and Bill's house. He took in a deep breath and looked at her with a bit of discomfort. Grabbing his hand she smiled and assured, "Don't worry! They're going to love you."

"Well, at least you're confident."

Before Elizabeth could knock on the door, Marta opened it. "Liz!" Without hesitation, they hugged and exchanged a cheek kiss. "And this must be that Angel I've heard so much about." Her southern accent was slight but still apparent and her short, semi-bobbed, white hair perfectly accentuated her strong jaw line and classy, but simplistic, style.

"Marta, I'd like you to meet Angel Martinez. Angel, this is my Aunt Marta."

Martinez smiled and put out his right hand to greet her properly.

"It's Marta, please." Reminding Elizabeth not to call her 'Aunt'. Though she was southern, she hated formalities. "And nonsense," she said, swatting away his hand as she wrapped her arms around his broad shoulders to hug him southern-style with a few pats on his back. Wanting to make a good first impression, he awkwardly reciprocated.

She backed up from him for a moment to get a good look at him. "Oh, my word! You are just as handsome as Liz described you to be. Come in, come in!" Marta gestured for them to enter. "Bill is out on the patio getting the grill started. I certainly hope you brought your appetite." She led them through the hall and into the kitchen where two sliding glass doors gave way to the patio with an encompassing view of the lake.

"You have a beautiful home." Martinez wasn't much for small talk but he had to make an effort.

"Why thank you!" Marta said as she opened the patio door. "Red, dear, our guests are here!"

Elizabeth walked over to the grill where Bill was violently brushing away the charred debris from his previous masterpiece. Looking up at her, Bill became excited. "Hey, baby girl!" He greeted her by swinging his left arm around her shoulder and kissing her hard on the cheek. Her face crinkled with schoolgirl delight as his tobacco-tinged mustache whiskers tickled her skin.

Breaking from his embrace, Elizabeth said, "Hey, Uncle Bill, this is -"

"Angel Martinez." His voice becoming more stern and crackling from years of cigarette smoke, he placed the grill brush to the side, wiped his hand on his apron, and forcefully shook Martinez's hand as he glared into his eyes. "Nice grip. We're off to a good start," he said as he patted Martinez on the shoulder while mid-handshake.

"Pleasure, Sir."

Appearing to inflate his already large chest, he advised, "Call me Bill. If I decide I like you later, you can call me Red."

Smiling with a head nod, Martinez said, "Fair enough, Bill."

"Have a seat. I just fired this bad boy up." Bill grabbed the brush again to clean the remaining debris from the grill. "Marta, honey, get the kids a beer. Liz, why don't you and your friend grab a seat? How do you take your steak, Martinez?"

"Oh, medium rare, please. Thank you."

Marta brought out a cold beer for everyone, including herself, and sat at the table across from Elizabeth. Bill placed four T-bone steaks on the grill; the meat sizzled as soon as it hit the flames and the aroma of garlic and Worcestershire sauce wafted in the air. Grabbing his beer, Bill took the chair directly across from Martinez.

"So, Martinez, you're a detective with SPD? Work any interesting cases lately?"

Rolling her eyes, Elizabeth said, "Uncle Bill, it's Saturday. Do we really have to talk shop?"

"Oh, come on, Liz. I've been out of the loop for a while. Can't you humor an old man?" He winked at her.

"Actually, I was just called out to a shooting last night,

South of the casino. Guy was robbed at his house and shot in the chest. Survived surprisingly. Claims $3,000.00 cash was taken. We're pretty sure it was drug related but we're still investigating, of course."

"Of course. So, how's Liz's case coming? You link that bastard that broke into her house to that asshole in prison?"

"Red!" yelled Marta. Elizabeth just shook her head and sighed.

"What? It's a valid question. I should've taken my pistol to that bastard years ago," he said as he took a swig of his beer.

"William Garret Redman!" yelled Marta as she smacked his arm. She turned to Martinez, "You will have to excuse him, dear. He doesn't really mean that."

"The hell I don't," he grunted. Marta smacked him again with a harsh look of disapproval.

Laughing, Martinez said, "Well, we did catch him a while back. Didn't Liz tell you? That case is over. He took a plea deal. Not by my choice."

"Damn city prosecutors. In the Corps, you couldn't get away with that shit. They would throw your ass in the brig for the smallest infraction and you would stay there until you got your act together. Keep your shit up and you would be dishonorably discharged after serving out your time. And us judge's advocates didn't hand out 'plea deals' like candy. Ruined a lot of young men's lives. Dumb Asses."

"You were in the Corps?"

Still seated, he saluted Martinez. "Retired. Colonel William Garrett Redman. At your service."

Instantly, Martinez pushed back his patio chair and stood at full attention, saluting Bill. "Corporal Angel Martinez. Sir!"

"As you were Corporal." He smiled and raised his beer.

In unison they clanged their beers as they yelled, "Oo-Rah!"

Getting up from his chair, Bill said, "Come on over here, Son. I'll show you how to make the meanest steak that ever crossed those lips of yours. And you can call me Red."

Bill and Martinez hammed it up as they finished the steaks while Marta and Elizabeth set the table and brought out the side dishes. When they finally sat down to eat, in the middle of the table was a smorgasbord of homemade pasta salad, in season sweet corn, grilled asparagus and steak grilled to perfection.

They all feasted as the men shared stories of their time in the Corps, talked about war, and manning up while the women spoke of sweet memories of time gone past and Elizabeth's favorite subject; her parents. Bill and Marta were special. They weren't just neighbors and good friends of her family. They *were* family. The only family she had now.

After cleaning up, they all said their good byes. "Thank you so much for having us," said Elizabeth as she hugged Marta tight.

"Martinez, you take care of her. I don't wanna have to

get my pistol out." Bill winked. "I'm sure we'll be seeing more of each other. Lot more stories to tell."

"I have no doubt. Red, it's been a pleasure," he said as he shook Bill's hand once more.

They walked the kids to the door and made them promise to come back soon. Elizabeth and Martinez waved one last time as they headed back toward her house down the wooded trail. Squeezing his hand, Elizabeth smiled. "Well, it seems you made quite an impression."

"Hey, you get two Marines in a room together and it's like a family reunion. They're nice people. I had a really good time. I didn't know you were related to them."

"Not technically. They're my Godparents. Bill and my dad went to law school together and remained friends ever since. Marta and my mom were practically inseparable. I've always called Bill my uncle. Marta has always wanted me to call her by her first name but she's more like a second mom to me than an aunt. They took care of everything after my parents died. I mean, they always consulted me but I left a lot to them. They're also my Trustees, until my next birthday anyway."

"Trustees? Sounds fancy. So you're a trust fund baby, huh?"

Loosening her grip on his hand and shooting him an offended look, she shot back at his words, "It's not as extravagant as it sounds."

"Whoa, I'm sorry. I didn't mean it that way." He grabbed her hand and stopped them both in their tracks.

Looking into her heavyhearted blue eyes he promised, "I'm sorry. Really. That was a stupid thing to say."

Trying to brush off his insensitivity, she turned away from him and began walking again. "Don't worry about it."

He hesitated before asking, "So, can I ask what happened to your parents? If it's an inappropriate question, just say so."

Knowing the question was inevitable she was prepared for it. "Well, when I should have been starting my second year in college, I was going through a trial. It actually went much faster than I expected from his arrest to the jury selection. But my dad had to keep putting off work and taking time off to make sure the prosecutor did 'her job correctly'."

"Marilyn?"

She sighed. "Yeah. I mean I understood, I guess. He was an attorney. Hell, he would have tried the case himself if he could've. Anyway, Steve was convicted and sent away in September of that year. My dad had this huge business trip planned right before the holidays and his partners warned if he didn't take care of things, they would begin the process of pushing him out.

I insisted he and my mom go. They both needed a break, you know? I did too. I mean, I had Marta and Bill here and I planned on going back to school the next semester. We all just needed a break. Plus, I didn't want to see everything my dad worked for his entire life just disappear because of me. I had caused enough problems for everyone - ”

Martinez cut her off like a mad driver in morning traffic. Grabbing her shoulders, he squeezed her hard but lovingly. “Liz, none of that was your fault.”

Tears welled in her eyes and began to trickle down her cheeks. “If they hadn’t gone away... if I didn’t insist...” she sniffled, “they wouldn’t have been driving – I tried to make things better and they just got worse.” She was almost embarrassed for breaking down the way she did.

He wrapped his arms around her and whispered in her ear yet again, “It wasn’t your fault, Liz.” He cupped her face in his hands, wiping away tears with his thumbs.

His brown eyes screamed safety and his lips parted invitingly. Elizabeth couldn’t resist a perfect moment to kiss him. Angel Martinez was by all accounts, heavenly. She pulled back and smiled, a tear hung in the corner of her eye before she swiped it with her forefinger.

Taking a deep breath, she pulled herself together. “Well then. Come on, our desert awaits.” Grabbing his hand again they walked until they reached her house. She led him down the embankment to the edge of the dock where two over sized pillows and a picnic basket awaited them. The sun was just beginning to set on the horizon giving the lake the most beautiful glow.

They sat down on the pillows and Elizabeth opened the chilled bottle of wine, pouring each of them a glass. Martinez looked back at the house, the screened in porch facing them. “Man, Liz. You have it made out here. Close neighbors but not too close. Lake view. Close enough to the city but again, not too close. It's so peaceful here."

"Yeah, it's home." She raised her glass, "Cheers," she said with a smile. She turned her gaze to the setting sun. "I've always loved the water. The lake in the summer, the ocean in the winter. My parents used to take me to the beach and swim with me. It was our favorite past time. It's the same comfort I feel while soaking in a warm bath. The water envelops you like a mother, lovingly swaddling her baby with a familiar blanket."

"I think that is the most poetic thing I've ever heard, Elizabeth Strong."

Giggling, she asked, "What do you know about poetry, Detective?"

"When you grow up in an orphanage, you find things to do. I read books. Every book I could find. Of course, that's where my friend, Chico, and me you remember the one at the FBI that helped me out with the Gardner case? That's when we first discovered Sherlock Holmes." He laughed at the memories. "We would end up literally fighting about who was going to be Holmes and who would be Watson. Of course, they're both fantastic characters."

"In-deed!" she responded mockingly.

Smiling with a bit of embarrassment himself this time, he reminded her, "There is not a single person on this earth who hasn't heard of Sherlock Holmes!"

"That couldn't possibly be a logical assessment, my dear Watson." She giggled again. "Okay, I'm done. I promise!" She couldn't help herself. His smile was perfection and his laugh made her warm in all the right places. When his smile disappeared and his expression turned more serious, she knew what was coming next.

"I know you don't want to talk about this..."

"Frankly, I don't. China already put her two cents in today. Are the two of you texting each other or something?"

"Come on, Liz. You have to consider this."

"No, Martinez, I don't. There is no reason for me to go to that hearing other than allow him to get one more dig at me. I have faith that he has not done a single thing that would make them let him out two years early."

Martinez became soft spoken, "Look, Liz, I need to tell you something and please don't get angry with me."

"Don't you realize that ending a statement with 'please don't get angry with me' is almost a guarantee that the person will get angry?" She pursed her lips flirtatiously.

"Can you just hear me out and try to keep an open mind?"

She sighed before sipping her wine. *He's not going to let it go, Liz. Just hear the man out.* "Okay, you win."

Looking down into his wine glass he began, "Back in June, after we arrested Johnnie Warren, I went to see Robinson." He stopped to gauge her emotion. Although she looked uncomfortable, he had her attention, so he continued. "Steve Robinson is not a man you want getting out of prison early. As it stands right now, he is a perfect candidate for early release. I believe you have a chance to throw a wrench in that. I've seen it happen before. I've talked to a few people about this and everyone says the same thing: Victim testimony at a parole hearing has a greater affect on the board than a written statement."

Elizabeth starred out at the horizon. The lake reflected the sun setting behind pink and lavender clouds on the pale blue sky. She knew he was right but she refused to give in. Sighing, she tried to convince him, "I know you mean well, but you don't understand. I just want to live and let live, ya know? Steve Robinson ripped my life apart six years ago. I don't want anything else to do with him. I don't want to go to that hearing and give him the satisfaction of knowing that I even still consider the fact he is a breathing organism worthy of any more of my time."

Martinez was growing frustrated. "He's going to get out and when he does, he is coming straight for you. 'Tell Lizzy, I'll see her soon.' His words, Liz."

Goose bumps formed on her arms.

"For crying out loud, the asshole had the nerve to call you three months ago and ask you to put in a good word for him at the hearing! He knew what was going on with Johnnie Warren. I *know* he was responsible! He-is-a-psychopath, Liz."

She met his glare. His eyes didn't move. He didn't blink. Grabbing her hand and interlocking his fingers with hers, he continued, "I have a plan. I just need your approval. I will drive you to the hearing and escort you. I'll stay with you through the entire hearing, Liz. You don't have to do this alone.

Investigator McMurphy has already approved everything; he's just waiting for an official request and confirmation so he can have everything set up. You have to at least try. This doesn't make you weak, this says to Robinson that you are truly done taking his shit and he can't get away with what he has done. We may not have had enough evidence to pin Johnnie Warren's actions on him, but you have every right to make your fears and concerns *and* hypothesis known to the parole board."

Taking a drink of her wine, she looked out to the sunset again. Before she could respond, her cell phone rang. *Damn it all to hell!*

"This is Elizabeth." Martinez watched her face turn serious as she listened to the voice on the other end. "I'll be there as soon as I can. Give me about fifteen minutes," she said before ending the call. "You know, I love that Marilyn brought in this new program for victims, but between the two of us being on call, I'm not sure this is working out so well!" She tilted her head flirtatiously and smiled when she met his gaze.

Smiling back at her, he assured her of his commitment. "Come on. I'll drive you myself. Then we can come back here and hopefully finish off with a quiet evening."

CHAPTER 3

Silverton, Ohio used to be a quiet little lake town, but between the ever-growing popularity of the amusement and water parks and the recently built casino, it was growing into quite the metropolis. Very different from the miles of cornfields, just upon the outskirts, with lingering scents of cow manure that Elizabeth used to know. Of course, some of those cornfields still existed, but they were few and far between.

They drove about ten minutes into town, to the new condos facing Lake Erie. It was a mile or so from Elizabeth's old apartment building. The flashing lights lit up the night sky and memories of moments past flickered through her mind. *Seriously?* Elizabeth and Martinez met up with the officer standing next to his cruiser. Officer Lucas shook his head and greeted Martinez with dissonance. "Detective, I don't believe we asked for assistance in this matter."

"You did not, Lucas. Just giving the lady a ride. You did call in a request for an advocate, did you not?"

Shaking his head in disbelief, Lucas refused to question authority. "Yep, sure did."

"Well, I'm just giving your victim advocate a ride here. You gotta problem with that?"

"Notta one."

"So, can you tell me what's going on, Officer Lucas?" asked Elizabeth.

Lucas glanced at Martinez, as if for approval, before continuing. "Got a call about twenty minutes ago. Female was distraught, asking for help, before the line went dead. It was a landline so dispatch was able to get a location. Seems husband and wife had an argument/altercation before husband decided to rip the phone out of the wall. Hence, here we are." Glancing at his notes he continued, "Husband is a Brandon DeFranco, wife is Pamela DeFranco. Officer Duval is speaking with the husband over there. Wife, Pamela, is upstairs in Unit 202 waiting for an advocate. She refuses to speak with us. You're on, Miss Strong."

Elizabeth walked up the stairs into the second floor lobby. She had not been in the old factory since they renovated and built the condos. *Wow,* she thought, *they really went all out. I wonder how much they get for these.* The door to the DeFranco residence was wide open and the light shone through into the dim hallway. Knocking on the door with her knuckles, she called out into the foyer,

"Mrs. DeFranco? I'm Elizabeth Strong, the advocate you asked for. Can I come in?"

She hesitated a moment before knocking again. "Mrs. DeFranco? Hello?" An average looking woman with shoulder-length brown hair turned around the corner to the edge of the foyer, dabbing her eyes with a tissue. She reminded Elizabeth of a teacher she had in high school.

"Mrs. DeFranco? Is it okay to come in?"

The woman didn't speak. She turned away and walked into the living room, slowly sitting down on the sofa. Assuming it was an invitation, Elizabeth walked in and sat down across from her in a leather recliner.

"My name is Elizabeth Strong. I'm a victim advocate with the Annapolis County Prosecutor's Office. I'm here to help in any way I can. Can you start by telling me what happened?"

Mrs. DeFranco was shaking slightly. To steady herself, she placed her elbows on her knees, and cupped her hands to her chin. Looking up to the high ceiling, tears welled up in the woman's eyes again as she periodically wiped her nose with a crumpled up tissue.

"Brandon and I have been married almost five years now. We're trying to have a baby." She sighed and a tear streamed down her right cheek. Her hands waved out beside her face. "I'm not quite sure when everything became so difficult!"

"Mrs. DeFranco, take your time."

She toughened up a bit and said, "Can you please call

me Pam? It's hard enough having all these strangers in my home due to all of this."

Elizabeth looked around the condo, noticing the Wok full of rice, vegetables, and meat, now strewn all over the sink and the cordless phone laying on the floor. It was apparent the phone dock had been ripped from its cord, which was still plugged into the wall, and the small table it sat on was toppled over.

Pam noticed Elizabeth's wondering eyes. She walked into the kitchen and started cleaning up the mess. "I made dinner. I usually don't do it much. He works a lot. Tonight, I expected him to come home earlier than he had. Unfortunately, he had a bad day and didn't feel much like eating. Of course, that led to an instant argument. I got upset with him and I threw it the sink. Immature, I know." She steadied herself on the counter and shook her head. "It just escalated from there. I said some things I shouldn't have and he just went off. He's been a little unsteady lately and I shouldn't have badgered him." Giving up on cleaning she tossed the pan back into the sink and began crying again.

"Whatever you said to him did not give him the right to make you fear for your safety. Especially not so much that you called the police for help."

After rinsing off her hands, she grabbed the dishtowel dangling from the oven handle. "So what happens now? I mean, God, what a mess I've created!"

It was a typical reaction, which Elizabeth was used to: Denial that there was a problem and regret for asking for help. "Pam, this wasn't your fault. The officers are downstairs with him. They are waiting on us. Either way, they will take him in and process him. Then there will be an arraignment Monday morning."

"But what if that isn't what I want?"

"Your husband disrupted a public service. When someone rips the phone out of the wall in the middle of a cry for help that is a crime. At this point neither one of you has a choice. So, you can either follow them to the station and wait for him to get an OR bond, or you can tell me you want a temporary protection order and he will not be allowed to return home for a while. Sometimes a period of cooling off is helpful. It can at least let you sort some things out, quietly, without having him breathing down your neck. Did he put his hands on you?"

"What's an OR bond?"

"That means he will get out on his own recognizance. You can pick him up at the station."

"I really think I need some time. He didn't touch me. He just frightened me. I mean he pushed me a little. I thought he might..."

"I'll tell you what, how about we all get out of your hair for the evening and give you the time you need. But you do need to decide if you want him home tonight. He can still get out, and he likely will, but you can request the temporary order for the rest of the weekend and we can revisit this on Monday morning when he shows up to court. Is that fair?"

"I need some time. But what if it makes it worse?"

"What if he comes home and the two of you pick up where you left off? Then we're right back to where we started."

She thought for a moment. "Will you be there Monday?"

Handing Pam her business card, Elizabeth looked at her empathetically and assured her, "I will be there until you decide you don't want me to be."

Hesitantly, she grasped the business card.

"Look, I know this is difficult, but I will help you get through this." She held onto the card before letting go and continued, "You don't have to do anything you don't want to do. *You're* in control here."

Pam nodded her head as if she understood and Elizabeth let go of the card. "Alright then. The only thing I need from you is your signature." Pulling some papers out of her purse, she placed them on the kitchen counter and explained the temporary protection order to Pam, handing her a pen. Noticing her apprehension, she added, "Remember, this is only temporary."

Signing the papers with tears in her eyes, Pam handed Elizabeth the pen and walked over to the sofa instantly mulling over her decision. Elizabeth felt guilty for leaving her. It was easy on her own turf in the courthouse; she had a job to do. Being in someone's home seemed more intrusive and much more difficult to just leave them in their own misery after such an occurrence. "I'll see you first thing Monday morning." She turned into the foyer and looked back, "Get some rest. Everything is going to be okay."

Heading back downstairs to meet the officers, Elizabeth was thankful they finally turned off the lights to the cruiser. Martinez met her at the end of the walkway.

"Everything good?"

Nodding affirmatively to his question, she looked at Lucas and then to Brandon DeFranco sitting patiently in the back of the cruiser. Attempting to hand Lucas the paperwork she said, "She's accepting the TPO until Monday. She needs a little time. If he's released on the OR, he can't come home tonight."

Looking at her with disdain he replied, "This can't possibly be filed on a Saturday night."

Martinez, knowing that was the wrong thing to say, took a step back and allowed Elizabeth's retort. Tilting her head a bit, the controlled look on her face became a slight growl. "Officer Lucas, though I'm not sure exactly what *your* procedure is once you get back to the department with this protection order, I'm pretty sure I know what procedure *I* am to follow and the law that backs it up." She shoved the paperwork at him, forcing him to accept it. "Like I said, he *cannot* come home tonight." She spun around and said to Martinez, "Let's go."

Flipping his keys in his hand, Martinez grinned, glanced over to Lucas and said, "You heard the lady." Hearing the passenger door close to his sedan, he walked to his vehicle and jumped in the driver's side, locking his seatbelt securely. He sat for a moment and gave Elizabeth a look of approval.

"What?" she asked, like a teenager defending her actions.

He laughed. "Hey, it's nothing. Really. Just..."

"Just, what?" She felt guilty for being so short with Lucas.

"Liz, it's okay. Lucas is a rookie but he's a good cop. He just needs a little help sometimes, as frustrating as that may be."

"I didn't mean to be pushy with him. But I'm sorry, he pissed me off. It's basic procedure he should be familiar with."

Throwing up his hands in defense he warned, "Hey! I'm on your side here! Lucas has been trained on the procedure. He shouldn't have questioned you. You did good, Liz. Seriously. I like your spunk." He turned the key to start the engine, put the car in drive, and gave her one last look before hitting the gas. "I've always liked your spunk, Elizabeth Strong."

They drove a few miles in silence. Martinez hated silence, unlike Elizabeth. "You know who that guy is, don't you?"

"Who? Brandon DeFranco, you mean?"

He laughed. "Yeah. Don't you read the Silverton Tribune?"

She rolled her eyes. "Don't you think we are bogged down with enough negativity in our lives?"

Staring at the dark road in front of them he lifted his

thumb from the steering wheel and replied, "I see your point. But seriously, don't be surprised if you're in next week's edition at some point. Brando DeFranco is a high-profile blogger/reporter for the Tribune. He writes about politics, crime, and most famously, anyone involved with the prosecutor's office or SPD. Not favorably, I might add. Just watch your step with this one. That's all I'm saying."

Fantastic! Just what I need to hear. "Are we sitting by the lake with a glass of wine yet?"

They finally hit Elizabeth's drive way, the gravel popping under the wheels to his sedan. Martinez pulled behind her tattered Beamer and put the vehicle in park. Elizabeth starred out to the dark sky for a moment before turning to him; the dim lighting highlighted the perfect sculpture of his chiseled face. Smiling she said, "Thanks for the ride."

His teeth illuminated from behind his perfect lips. "Anytime. I hope this doesn't mean our date is over?"

She was a little embarrassed for suggesting it. "No! Of course not." She grabbed the handle to the car door, "Come on. I have a plan for the rest of the evening. Well, as long as I don't get another call."

He began to follow her back into the house. "I'm hoping the chances are slim to none." As soon as her back was turned, he placed his hands together under his chin, looked up to the sky, and silently prayed he was right.

After hanging her bag on the back of a dining chair, she ventured into the living room and lit a few candles, though she wished it was cold enough outside to burn a fire in the fire place. *It'll be winter soon enough*, she thought. She hadn't changed the place much since moving in. Although she did buy new furniture, the sofa and love seat still created an L shape in front of the fire place and her mother's blanket hung comfortably over the back of the new sofa. The television remained in the corner surrounded by shelves of vinyl records. Her father's old multi-record turntable, however, was accentuated by her Bose stereo system where she could play music for hours on end.

She reached the opposite end of the room, knelt down in front of the alphabetized collection, and pulled out The Beatles compilation album, "Hey Jude", from 1970. Carefully extracting the record from its jacket, she twirled it between her fingers to Side Two, where her favorite songs anxiously awaited the needle to be nestled upon them. Martinez made himself comfortable on the edge of the sofa and watched her every move. She turned to him before laying the album on the turntable and said, "The only time I know of that a needle is actually welcomed."

He looked at her a tad awkward. With the record suspended between her middle fingers and her thumbs, "Sorry," she defended, "Just a little criminal-justice-humor. Too much?"

Looking down to the floor as he shook his head and sighed, he looked back up and gazed at her, "Where have you been all my life?"

Giving him a sexy smirk, she set the album carefully on the revolving platter and placed the needle gently on the first groove. "Hey Jude" began to play and Elizabeth turned up the volume until they could hear nothing but the music. She stood up, turned to him, and graciously placed her right hand in front of him as an invitation.

Without saying a word, he gently took her hand and stood up to meet her. Interlocking his fingers with hers, he wrapped his right arm around her tiny waist, almost possessively, and drew her body in close to him. They swayed to the music, ingesting invisible pheromones in the air. His lips brushed her neck sending waves of electricity through every inch of her being. Before the song had ended, they had made their way into her bedroom.

The nervous tension in her stomach battled the every-growing desire to be consumed by him. She whispered with shame, "It's been a long time."

He gently kissed her lips and looked into her deep blue eyes. "Remember, you're in charge here, Liz. You're the boss."

If ever three little words had won a war...

WITH THE BLANKETS strewn and windows fogged, they laid on their backs in a satisfied stupor, as if a bright white light had passed between them.

Elizabeth grabbed a red throw from the floor leaving him the sheet. She wrapped it around herself and leaned over to him. "Can I get you something to drink?"

Placing the hair that had fallen onto her face behind her ear, he replied, "A water would be great."

She smiled, kissed him hard on the lips, and jumped off the bed, nearly skipping into the kitchen. Her legs shook at the weight of her body. She reached the counter and steadied herself. *Holy Orgasm, Batman!* The shaking subsided with a good stretch of her hamstrings. Reaching into the refrigerator, she debated whether she needed water to hydrate herself, or a glass of wine to help calm her down. She decided both were necessities at this point.

Elizabeth returned to her room where Martinez had his head propped up on a pillow with one arm behind his head; the sheet modestly covering the necessary extremities like a Demigod. Wine glass in one hand, water bottle in the other, her blanket unraveled itself from its tie and fell to the floor.

"Shit!" she exclaimed as she fumbled to place the drinks on the nightstand and cover herself again.

"Well, it's a little late to be shy, don't you think?" He said seductively.

Good point. She covered herself up anyway and smiled. She handed him the water and sat down on the bed next to him. She left the wine on the nightstand and reached out for the water once he took a big swig.

Looking at her awkwardly, he asked, "So, I have to share now?"

She was taken aback. "I think we've shared much more than water tonight, don't you think?"

"Touché." He ran his eyes over her, sighed with pleasure, and made himself comfortable again.

Bending over him, she kissed his forehead and whispered, "I'll be back in a bit."

Instantly, his sleep deprivation wore off. "Where you going?"

"I'm just going to sit on the porch and look a couple things up online."

"Awe come on, Liz. Lay with me..."

After taking a sip of her wine she ran her fingers over his smooth bare chest. "Did you know the Pagans believed that the women, after ritualistically having sex with their men, stole their energy from them in order to conduct magic at night?"

He was stunned by her analogy. "Are you telling me you're a witch, Elizabeth Strong?" Jumping up from his comfort, he grabbed her by the shoulder with one hand while placing the palm of his other hand on her forehead. His voice became deep and hysterically frightening. "Be damned you flagrant devil woman from hell!"

The wine spilled down her breasts and soaked the blanket, her laughter sharply shaking the room. Still laughing, she placed her half-empty glass on the nightstand.

He lunged at her, covering her body with his massive presence. "What is this evil you speak?"

She couldn't contain her laughter. "Oh my God, you freaking ogre!" She pushed him away and he conceded. "See that, Mr. Detective. I'm stronger than you think."

His smile was pure delight against his light brown skin. "Don't be long, okay? I'm afraid of the dark." He winked and rolled over, stuffing the down pillow under his head.

It had been years since she felt so energized. She grabbed her laptop from the living room, filled her wine glass, and ventured to the screened in porch. She left the door open, but careful not to disturb her sleeping Angel. Placing her laptop and wine on the wicker table in front of her, she opened the screen, a band-aid staring at her where the camera once did. She turned on the airport and went straight to Google, typing in 'Brandon DeFranco, Silverton Tribune'.

The results popped up on the screen. "Damn," she quietly said to herself. "Busy guy." The headlines all appeared political to some extent.

"SILVERTON POLICE FOLLOWING A TREND OF MILITARIZATION?"

"SPD OFFICER IN HOT WATER AGAIN"

"NEW VICTIM ASSISTANCE PROGRAM, TOO MUCH?"

WHAT THE HELL? Upon reading the title, she immediately clicked on the article.

. . .

"ANNAPOLIS COUNTY'S Victim Assistance Program recently introduced a new service to victims of crime: Specifically for victims of domestic violence and rape. In previous years, a victim advocate would meet the alleged victim in court on the day of the defendant's arraignment. The victim would then be entitled to a temporary protection order as well as being informed of the general court process.

WITH THE HELP of government funds, aka Annapolis County's taxpayer dollars, victims of crime can now summon an advocate once the police are dispatched to and reach the scene of a crime. While many argue these services are necessary, some say it is open for debate.

STATISTICALLY, the number of protection orders granted at arraignments is quite low compared to the number of crimes committed, which would be eligible for such government assistance. Alternatively, the number of protection orders that are actually granted at the time of arraignment and subsequently dropped one week later, are outrageous. (Source)

ALTHOUGH THESE SERVICES are offered to all victims of crime, the Prosecutor's Office claims that the majority of its use will likely come from victims of domestic violence.

Ironically enough, this is the one crime in which victims typically request the order, then subsequently drop it within days of charges being filed."

WELL, no shit, Sherlock! Elizabeth was so frustrated she slammed the computer screen shut, grabbing her wine glass for a sip of calm. It was mind boggling to her that so many people in the 21st century still were not educated on the facets of domestic violence. When women and men alike were assailed by a loved one, at the time of the attack they're frightened enough to call the police and request a protection order. Once the reality set in, they were even more terrified the abuse would worsen at the mere fact of the protection order. And it sometimes did.

Elizabeth knew all too well that a piece of paper wouldn't keep someone at bay. Not someone who was bound and determined to unleash his or her power over the other individual in every way possible. These people were already rule breakers. They didn't give a rat's ass about a 500-foot invisible line. But, if it gave a battered woman one good nights rest, she was ready to be there to help make sure it was enforced.

Frustrated, she finished her wine as she walked into the kitchen. She turned on the faucet and rinsed out her glass, setting it on the counter. Staring out of the window above the sink she thought, *Nice job, Brandon DeFranco. Nothing like an article from a 'reputable' source to force people to focus on something other than the real problem.*

She walked back through the dining area and stopped at the doorway to her bedroom. All the negative thoughts dissipated as she watched Martinez sleeping in her bed. The cool lake breeze gently swung the sheer curtains from side to side. Turning out the light on the nightstand, she crept into the bed, trying not to disturb him. As soon as she was comfortable, he rolled over, spooning her from behind and cradling her breasts with his arm. Safety: A luxury unknown to her for some time.

"I'll go to the hearing," she whispered.

He pulled her closer to him and rested his cheek at the nape of her neck. "And I'll be right next to you the whole time."

CHAPTER 4

$\mathcal{E}$lizabeth had never felt so good pulling into the parking garage before work on a Monday morning. Reaching her spot and putting her Beamer in park, China was sitting in the driver's seat of her car in the adjoining space, finishing her cigarette. Looking at each other, Elizabeth's eyes widened and she smiled, mouth open, as she waved excitedly. She pulled the keys out of the ignition, barely making it out of the door fast enough to jump in the passenger side of China's Buick.

In unison, they cheered, "Good morning!"

Becoming skeptical, she lifted her chin, squinted her eyes sideways, and deviously grinned, "You had bacon and eggs yesterday morning didn't you?"

Elizabeth pulled her shoulder bag into her stomach and tilted her head back as she drew in a deep breath and released it as if savoring the smell of a freshly mowed lawn.

"Oh my God. Oh-my-God! - Hot damn! It's about time. So…" egging her on for all the dirty details.

Taking another deep breath, she explained, "I have never felt anything like it in my entire life. And that's the God's honest truth."

"Day-um… Oh, Liz. Oh, honey," China said. The look on her face became worrisome. "Maybe you should've stayed a vegetarian."

Elizabeth slapped her forearm, "Really, China? You've been pushing this for months. 'Little sausage gravy on your biscuit,'" she laughed.

Her eyes widened, "You've already fallen for the guy. Holy shit. That man *must* be an Angel to have won over Elizabeth Strong." Her face turned serious. "He better not hurt you."

"Oh come on, it's more likely I'll hurt myself, right?"

"Cop or no cop, I will cut him, Liz."

The windows were down, causing Elizabeth to look around in every direction. "Don't say that too loud, China!"

"Oh, stop being so paranoid." She took one last drag of her cigarette and turned to her like a childhood defender. "Seriously, I will cut a bitch," she said flicking her cigarette out the car window.

"Don't be so dramatic."

"Hey, I just said you should have sex with the man, not fall in love with him."

"I'll have you know he talked me into going to the hearing."

China's mouth dropped a little, "Well I'll be damned."

"He's going with me. Said he is setting it all up. He'll be with me the whole time."

"Okay. Impressive. I'm just saying cops are a different breed, Liz. I have one word for you, Thomas."

Pursing her lips and grabbing the door handle she retorted, "Oh, Thomas is a different breed alright. Remember, not all cops are cheating assholes, either."

China rolled her eyes as she exited the vehicle. They walked to the automatic sliding doors and Elizabeth hit the oversized button on the wall forcing the doors to separate, allowing them entry. Their heels clanked on the tile floor as they made it to the elevator. Elizabeth pushed the button for the fourth floor and the doors began to close.

"So, how was your date with the mysterious Chester?"

Leaning her back against the glass wall opposite the elevator door she sighed, "God, don't even ask."

"Oh, come on. The other day you were singing the man praises and telling me I should be happy for you."

"Yeah, well, that was until he mentioned marriage."

"What? Get the hell outta here!"

"I kid you not. One minute we're sitting there enjoying the best lasagna I ever put to my lips; all I could think about was ripping his clothes off, slathering his body with pasta sauce, and having myself one big cannoli for desert, right? The next minute he's talking about getting married and having kids. *Kids*, Liz! The man has lost his damn mind."

The bell dinged to remind them they made it to the fourth floor. As the doors opened, they exited and headed down the hall toward the office. China continued, "We managed to make it back to my place, he drove after all, did our thing and I rushed him out the door quick as I could. He didn't seem too happy about that."

Shaking her head and giggling slightly, Elizabeth said, "Well, I would imagine anyone would have a problem with that. He did just take you out to dinner."

China punched in the code on the hefty door to the prosecutor's office. "Maybe on his next date after only a few months he won't bring up kids. Frigin' amateur." She pushed the door open and held it for Elizabeth. The scent of fresh coffee and bagels drifted through the air. Walking past Marilyn's office and exchanging 'Good morning' with the office manager, they stopped in the middle of the main office near Constance's desk to take a peak at the goodies.

"Who brought bagels?" asked Elizabeth.

"Who cares? It's breakfast," said China.

Constance, one of the main secretaries, turned around from her position at her desk and smiled. "I did. Enjoy! I think you're gonna need it." She winked, whirled her chair back around to her computer, and started typing again.

Disconcerted, Elizabeth said, "Thanks. I think," and turned to China who shrugged her shoulders as she stuck a cinnamon bagel in her mouth so she could pour herself a cup of coffee.

Mildred made her way from the back end of the office.

"Good morning ladies! It's been interesting for sure!" Her red shoes nearly matched the color of her short spunky hair.

"Mildred, I just love your shoes! Are they new?" Elizabeth loved Mildred and always complimented her unique styles.

"Oh, no. I picked these little gems up last year. But thank you! By the way, as you can see, the office is a buzz this morning..."

Elizabeth looked to her left then her right as she slapped cream cheese on her bagel, "I see that. What's going on anyway?" she asked before stuffing her mouth with a bite of the toasted asiago cheese crust.

Stomping a foot on the ground and rolling her eyes she confessed, "I just can't believe no one, especially you girls, didn't know this was coming. Marilyn acts as if none of us need to be a part of anything around here!"

"Mildred, spit it out."

Looking down the hall, Mildred motioned to Marilyn who was speaking with a short, stocky, blonde as if she was giving her a tour of the place. "*That* is what's going on," she said snidely.

China pushed her way into the conversation. She took a sip of her coffee to wash down the cream cheese on the roof of her mouth, "Who's that?"

Mildred's eyes went from China, to Elizabeth, and back to Marilyn and the other woman. She crossed her arms on her chest, tilted her head aggravatingly, and tapped her toe on the carpet, "That is your new director of victim services, ladies."

China and Elizabeth's thoughts were corresponding and mutually vocal. "Oooh-*shiiit...*"

Making their way down the hall, Marilyn made eye contact. Mildred smiled at her and returned to her desk before Marilyn could speak, "Good morning, ladies. I'd like to introduce you to Peggy Cabot. Peggy, this is Elizabeth Strong and Mia Lee, or China as we call her. Our two advocates you'll be working with."

After exchanging handshakes and nice-to-meet-you's, China quickly and defensively added, "It's Mia. Welcome aboard."

"Elizabeth handles all the domestic violence cases, China -"

Giving Marilyn a strong look she interrupted, "Mia..." In China's mind, you had to earn the right to call her by her nickname.

"Sorry, *Mi-a*, handles everything else. The rape cases have been split between the two. Of course, until now." Marilyn took a breath before continuing, "So, ladies, Peggy will be taking over the victim services department as well as all the rape cases. You will be reporting to her from here on out. I know this may come as a bit of a surprise, however, you're also aware we have been considering this for some time..."

They continued to listen, as if interested, nodding and smiling fictitiously while eyeing up their new boss. China looked over at Elizabeth, her slanted eyes widening and narrowing at each statement careful not to be noticeably rude. Elizabeth continued to smile as Marilyn spoke, forcefully containing her laughter.

Giving her throat lubrication with a sip of coffee after Marilyn seemed to finish, Elizabeth said, "Welcome aboard, Peggy. Look forward to working with you. We have a busy morning, so, we should probably get ready to go to court."

Agreeing, China tipped her coffee mug at Peggy and walked back to her office. Elizabeth followed behind her. Making it to her office, Elizabeth turned on the computer and pulled up the morning docket. China slipped in and sat in one of the chairs in front of Elizabeth's desk. Nestling her coffee cup in her lap, she leaned forward, "What-in-the-Sam-Hell?"

Trying not to be negative, Elizabeth sighed, "We knew this was coming right? I mean, I didn't think it would be today! But we knew this was coming."

"Liz, as if Marilyn wasn't bad enough, now we get Cankles?"

Drawing her eyebrows together and squinting she asked, "Cankles? What the hell is that?"

"Cankles, you know, when your calf muscle literally blends in with your ankles? Frigin' Cankles!" She laughed out loud from deep within her belly and Elizabeth cautiously joined her. "Seriously, that woman should *not* be wearing a skirt."

"Oh my God! You are entirely too much. Okay, I need to get this docket printed and get over to court. I had a call out Saturday night, and I really should get there early. I have a feeling she is going to want to drop the protection order first thing."

Rolling her eyes as she stood up, China said, "Really? Imagine that!" She stood in the doorway and held her mug of coffee nonchalantly. "So, what was the Saturday drama anyway?"

Before Elizabeth could answer they heard footsteps coming down the hall. China peeked across her shoulder and saw Peggy coming. Turning back to look at Elizabeth, she rolled her eyes and sighed.

Peggy stopped in front of Elizabeth's office and in a nasally, snobbish voice said, "Ladies..." China and Elizabeth looked at each other with mutual discomfort. Either completely ignorant or oblivious to their discontent, she continued, "I'd really like to meet with you both so I can go over some things. Can you please follow me to my office?"

They looked at each other once more. China crossed her eyes out of Peggy's sight and Elizabeth bit the inside of her lip to keep from giggling. Being the brave one, China spoke up, "Sorry, Peggy. Docket starts at nine o'clock sharp. Gotta get going!" She winked at Elizabeth, spun on her heel, and returned to her own office to grab her things for court.

Peggy stood at the doorway, a tad shocked, her eyes going back and forth between the two of them before landing on Elizabeth. Shrugging, Elizabeth honestly explained, "Sorry. The judge doesn't like us to be late."

Looking down her nose she responded, "Then I would like you both in my office after court."

Geeze lady, it's your first day. "Well, see, we usually grab lunch right after court. Monday dockets are pretty full and take up the entire morning."

"Good, that means we can have lunch together, get to know each other a bit and I can fill you in on the changes taking -"

"Sorry, Peggy. Our lunch hour is unpaid." She grabbed her docket from the printer and stuffed it in her bag. "I'm sure we should have some time to meet up after lunch," she said, spitting a smile at Peggy as she swiftly passed by her to leave. "Can't keep Judge Bennett waiting!"

Crossing her arms, Peggy was perturbed and left in the dust.

JUDGE BENNETT WAS TYPICALLY LATE, but he was the only one allowed to do so. Elizabeth and China waited patiently in his chambers until he decided to grace them with his presence. At 9:05 am the door finally swung open, "Good Monday morning, Ladies. How was your weekend?" asked the Judge.

China laughed and sarcastically answered, "Spectacular, Judge. And you?"

Opening the closet door, he reached for his robe on the hook and placed it over his head. Pulling it down over his tie he smiled as he claimed, "It was memorable."

Lacing her fingers together and setting them on her knees, China lit up with interest. "Ah, do tell, your Honor!"

"A gentleman never kisses and tells my dear."

There was a knock at the door from the clerk's side and then it opened. "Hey, Liz, there's a Pamela DeFranco out here that needs to speak with you."

Grabbing her bag she gave a half grin, "Here we go!"

Judge Bennett held the courtroom door open and waved China through. She reluctantly began walking into the courtroom. "Come on Judge, don't leave a girl guessing," she whispered.

The court bailiff stood from his position as China walked to her seat at the table at the front of the courtroom and the Judge made his way to the bench, still smiling as China prodded for information.

"All rise."

ELIZABETH FOUND Pam sitting on the wooden bench in the lobby. Hearing the shoe heels click on the marble flooring made her stand to meet Elizabeth. She seemed anxious and timid.

"How are you doing this morning, Pam?" she asked as she took a seat on the bench.

Seemingly frazzled, she sat next to Elizabeth gripping papers to her chest. "I'm really not sure. I – I'm not sure about anything anymore." Her brown hair was neat and her clothing, schoolteacher appropriate. She was casually average. Her face was more that of a frightened deer.

"Did your husband obey the order from Saturday?"

Shutting her eyes for a moment and breathing deeply, she nodded her head. "His 'friend', Samantha, called Saturday night wanting to know what was going on. They work together." She rolled her eyes. "He stayed with her the rest of the weekend and she was bringing him today. They may already be here."

Approvingly shaking her head, Elizabeth continued, "Okay, good. Once his case is called, we will go in front of the judge, he will go over the charges, explain both of your rights, and Brandon will enter his plea. Before we go up there, you need to decide if you want to continue the protection order. The order is only temporary and ends once the case is over. If you decide that you want something more concrete, we will need to go over to Common Pleas Court and request a Civil Protection Order. That order can last for five years. Have you given any thought to - "

Pam cut her off and handed Elizabeth the papers she had been gripping. "I found this yesterday as I was gathering some things for his co-worker to take to her house for him."

Taking the papers from her, Elizabeth's eyes grew as she read the first page, "Psychological Evaluation of Brandon J. DeFranco, by Warren D. Frasier, MD." She looked up at Pam and sighed, "Wow."

Looking over her shoulder and trying not to attract

any attention to their conversation, her voice trembled as she whispered, "I didn't even know he was seeing anyone!"

"Have you read through this?"

"I did... Elizabeth, that is not the man I married." A tear fell down her cheek as she turned her sad brown eyes to the large glass windows facing the busy street outside.

Frustrated but eager to help, Elizabeth reached out and gently touched Pam's forearm, "Hey, everything's going to be okay. One step at a time. I'll be right here through this entire process." She reached in her bag and grabbed a tissue, handing it to the woman. "I have to get in the courtroom now. When the Judge calls his name, come up to the bench and stand beside me. You don't have to say a word to him. I'll be there and the bailiff will be there, okay? I have a few other cases as well, but I promise I will take a look at this first chance I get," she said, stuffing the evaluation in her file folder.

"Thank you, Elizabeth."

MARTINEZ SAT at his desk typing up a request to Investigator McMurphy at Mansfield Prison. The parole hearing was scheduled for Thursday afternoon and it was imperative the request be sent in as soon as possible. Detective Shawn Johnson looked up over the partition at Martinez. "Whatcha working on?"

Leaning back in his chair and lacing his fingers behind his neck he replied, "Well, Liz decided to go to the parole hearing, so I'm trying to get this request done to send in to Investigator McMurphy down at Mansfield. He's going to set it all up for me to escort her."

Shawn looked impressed, "Wow, how did you talk her into that?"

Placing his fingers back on the keyboard after stretching out his bulging triceps, he winked, "Wouldn't you like to know."

"I would! You know I live vicariously through you, man." He rolled his eyes as he shook his head and grinned before picking up the receiver of his phone to make a call. After dialing a number and getting a busy signal, he hung up. Rubbing the day old, salt and pepper scruff on his chin, he asked, "So she's really gonna give a statement, huh?"

Biting his bottom lip and releasing it, he replied, "She is." He tilted his head to the side, "You know, if it helps in the least to keep that asshole behind bars for another two years, it will be worth it." He paused for a moment. "You worked that case. I would think you of all people would be vying against his release."

"Sure, I worked on the case, but it was more of a behind the scenes. I didn't actually work with Strong. I doubt we even crossed paths through the duration. I just remember a lot and we talked about it amongst ourselves quite a bit; it was a huge case that we were all involved in to some extent." He laughed and scrubbed through his cropped hair, "Caused a lot of these premature gray hairs!"

Nodding, as if he understood, Martinez said, "I hear ya, man."

They could hear Chief John Holden's footsteps coming down the hall. Johnson looked towards the door and Martinez turned in his chair to face Holden looming in the doorway, nearly taking up the entire space. Still studying the papers in his hand, he cleared his throat, "Morning, you guys have a good weekend?"

"I wish I could say mine was as good as Martinez," belted Shawn. He winked when Martinez glanced his way.

"Well, you're about to have a better morning than he is, so call it even." Handing Martinez the paper, his grey eyes peered at him through the top of his black-framed glasses. "Just got our warrant on the suspect from Friday's shooting. I need you to get over there ASAP. Take Lucas and Duval with you."

"Nice! Can I just finish this up before I go?" he asked pointing to his computer screen.

"Sorry, you have time to grab your keys on this one Martinez. Boys are waiting for you downstairs. I'm afraid your entire day is going to be tied up. I don't want this served until the suspect is seen going in or coming out of the residence. This is too sensitive."

Frustrated, Martinez grabbed his keys and stood from his chair. "Hey Johnson? I really need you to do something for me."

"I got your six..."

He started out the door. "Email this request over to McMurphy for me? It *has* to get to him today."

Shawn lifted his hand in the air over the partition and gave Martinez a thumbs up.

Scurrying out the door, Martinez hollered down the hall, "I owe you one!"

"You owe me more than one, Martinez!" Shawn shook his head and raised himself from his desk, slithering into Martinez's seat. He placed his elbow on the desk and gripped his chin, glancing over the document he was now responsible for. He uploaded the document to the draft email Martinez had ready. Using the mouse, he hovered over the send button before clicking it.

"Johnson..." Chief Holden's voice was deep and demanding.

His heart skipping a beat, Shawn turned to see Holden standing back in the doorway. "Damn, Chief, give a guy a heart attack why don't you!"

"I need you to get over to Filmore Street. Got another possible OD." He glared into Shawn's eyes. "I want whoever is selling this shit in my city." He breathed heavy through his nostrils and shook his head before returning to his office.

Shawn visually followed the chief until he was out of sight again and turned back to the computer screen, clicking a few buttons with the mouse. He picked his cell phone from his front pocket and pulled up a contact, sending a text message that read 'You owe me BIG.'

STANDING in line at Jared's Java House waiting to order, Elizabeth sighed as she said to China, "You know, I don't understand why the judge is scheduling these pretrials so soon after the arraignments."

"What do you mean?" she asked as her eyes scoured the menu written on the large chalkboard behind the counter.

"The pretrial for DeFranco is in two days. The parole hearing is that afternoon!"

"Eew. Fun day. Why didn't you just take the day off for that?"

"No time to ask. Not that it matters. I don't know. Maybe I'm just looking for an excuse to get out of going."

Pursing her lips and scrunching her brows together, China gave her a look of disapproval, "Umm, no." She glanced back to the menu and sighed with indecision. "Should I get the chicken salad or the egg salad? Egg salad might make me too gassy."

Chuckling, Elizabeth made her way to the counter. "Hi Kathy, how you doing today?"

She ripped the previous order from her tablet. "Ladies! How are you? It's been busy! Gimme just a sec, okay?" She turned the order into the kitchen window behind her and spun back around to the counter, her long blonde ponytail following. "So, what can I get you ladies today?"

They both ordered the special brew of the day and a sandwich before finding a table for two in the lunch madness. Swinging her purse over the shoulder of the chair, China sat down heavily. "There has seriously got to be a better way!"

"No kidding. But until one of us thinks of what that might be, we're stuck with this." Pulling out her court folder she flipped through to the assessment Pam DeFranco gave her. She leaned in over the table and spoke quietly, "Pam gave this to me at court. It's a mental assessment from her husband's doctor, of which she had no idea he was seeing!"

"Ooh, juicy! Have you read it?"

"Not yet. I skimmed through it. He sounds like a freaking psycho."

"Okay, if you're not going to bring it up... What-in-the-hell is with this Peggy Cabot character?"

Tilting her head back and twisting her neck around, she locked eyes with China and shook her head. "I don't know. I wish Marilyn would have given us a little heads up. I'm not happy that we now have to report to two people. And I'm even less happy she's already trying to call a meeting on her first day. I mean, she could at least feel things out before demanding we have lunch with her. Seems a little presumptuous."

"Try pretentious. The woman literally talked through her nose. I heard she's from Beachwood. Fancy smanchy." She rolled her eyes. "Whatever."

"I guess the upside is we won't be taking the rape pager home anymore and in my eyes, not gonna be missed! Those cases are even more frustrating to deal with."

"Oh, they weren't that bad."

"Really China? What about that time we both got called out because there were two girls, first thing in the morning. Remember? They looked like they were both hung over, completely drugged out, and could give a rat's ass about talking to us. Looked as if they just pulled an all night train and simply wanted to be sure they didn't get an STD or wind up pregnant the next month! God, that was awful."

Cupping her hand over her mouth to keep from spitting her coffee out, China continued the trip down memory lane. "What about the time you had that girl who said she was raped in the park and she had her monthly visitor? You had to sit through the *entire* exam with her."

Elizabeth's gag reflux got the best of her remembering the stench in the air that day. She gulped down the bite of her wrap she just took; it slid hard down her throat. "Ugh, damn you, China!"

She laughed so hard tears formed in the corner of her eyes. "I'm sorry!" Still laughing and grabbing her chest she confessed, "I couldn't resist! Hey, at least Cankles can deal with all that shit from now on, right?"

"Exactly my point. Of course we'll still have to deal with people like Phil and his girlfriend who decided to brand him with a hot iron."

"Oh my God! That poor man." China took a deep breath and looked out the window fantasizing, "That poor, sexy man. I wonder if that left a scar?"

"The man was wearing a wife-beater, in court, so cloth

would not stick to his skin. You could literally see the shape of an iron on his back. I'm pretty sure it left a scar."

CHAPTER 5

Knowing it was going to be a stressful day, Elizabeth popped a Valium upon waking up. The bottle of wine she drank the night before didn't keep her from tossing and turning. At least her failure to sleep had kept the nightmares at bay. Hearing China's shoes clunking down the hallway, she focused her eyes on the doorway.

"Good morning sunshine!" China said. She made herself comfortable and flung her oversized bag in the chair next to her as she sat down. "You would not believe the night I had!" She placed her coffee cup on the desk and fumbled around in her purse as she continued, "You have to read these texts. Chester was blowing my phone up yesterday. The man has totally gone postal."

Elizabeth leaned back in her office chair holding her coffee mug with both hands and waited patiently with heavy eyes as China scrolled through her phone to reveal her latest drama.

"5:02 pm; 'Hope you had a good day!' 5:29 pm; 'Thinking about you, call me.' 6:13 pm; 'I hope I didn't do something wrong.' 8:00 pm; 'I really miss talking with you. Please call.' What the hell?" Her voice begged for help.

Squinting her eyes and taking a deep breath, Elizabeth was unsure on how to respond. Appearing as if she sucked on a lemon, she looked China square in her eyes and said, "Yikes."

"Yikes? Yikes is all you have for this?" Sighing, China threw her phone in her purse and grabbed her coffee cup from the desk taking a sip. She looked at Elizabeth closely, "Damn, Liz, you look like shit."

"Why, thank you, China."

"Oh honey, I'm sorry," she said realizing her selfishness. "Are you doin' okay?"

Setting her cup down in front of her, she confessed, "Honestly, I just want this day over with."

China stared into the bottom of her cup and looked up, rolling her eyes. "I'm sorry, I shouldn't have bombarded you with my trivial bullshit."

She shook her head and smiled. "No worries. And it's not trivial by any means. I'm sorry, I just didn't get any sleep. I'm thinking about this pretrial, I'm totally considering skipping this whole parole hearing, and Peggy has called a mandatory meeting first thing tomorrow morning!"

Her body became stiff and she perked up abruptly. "Mandatory meeting? What the -"

"Um, yeah. She's on the warpath. You thought Marilyn was bad? Get ready for Marilyn 2 point O. I seriously don't have time for this."

"Okay, first of all, the pretrial? Cakewalk. Who cares about the little girl who married the wrong guy? Lesson learned - or not. Not your problem, Liz. Second of all, the parole hearing? You're going. No questions asked. Okay? Done deal. Martinez will be there, nothing to worry about. And Peggy? Screw her! Mandatory meeting. Pfft. Whatever," she said with a wave of the hand.

Wishing she had an ounce of China's confidence, she starred off into space like a frightened teenager ready to give a public speech in front of her entire graduating class for the first time.

Demanding her attention, China reiterated her position, "Liz, you got this."

THE DOCKET WAS PRETTY light on Thursday. It seemed not many people committed crimes midweek. Judge Bennett typically scheduled pretrials on these days, although there were a few stragglers in for their arraignments. As China dealt with an aggressive storeowner looking to hang a thief over ten dollars, Elizabeth sat in the corner of the lobby reading the mental evaluation of Brandon

DeFranco. The further she read, the more concerned she became for Pam.

The city prosecutor, Lydia Hamilton, walked through the lobby towards Elizabeth. Her pale skin accentuated her curly, strawberry blonde hair and hazel eyes. "Good morning, Liz!"

"How are you, Lydia?"

"Ready to get these pretrials over with. I leave for vacation this evening and I still haven't even packed!"

She stood up to meet her properly. "Going anywhere fun?"

Her eyes brightened at the thought. "Cancun."

"Nice! I always wanted to go there. Maybe one of these days."

Lydia grasped her files close to her chest, "This is our second year. It is absolutely fabulous. You really have to go." Looking over at China who was speaking with a crime victim, she asked, "Old man Kriems is at it again, huh?"

She shook her head empathetically. "That poor man has some kind of theft every week. It must be hard at his age still trying to run a store. Hey, we have a pretrial for the DeFranco's. I was hoping we could get started as soon as possible because I need to leave by 11:00 am."

"Of course! Follow me to the judge's chambers and we'll get started right now. Is your victim here?"

"I haven't checked the courtroom yet, but I know she'll be here. I'll scope it out and meet you in chambers."

Standing with an aura of confidence, she looked at her

watch and back to Elizabeth, "We'll get you outta here in time. I'll see you in there." She smiled and continued on her path. As soon as Lydia was out of sight, Shawn Johnson came through the metal door connecting the police station to the courthouse. Scurrying over towards her, he reached out and tapped her shoulder. "Hey..."

Elizabeth jumped and shrieked like a child afraid of the monster in the closet. Grabbing her chest and breathing a sigh of relief she giggled, "Shit! Sorry, I'm a little jumpy today."

"My fault. I didn't mean to startle you. Do you have a sec? Martinez said I might be able to find you here."

Looking at her phone she paused, "I guess so. But I need to get to a pretrial soon."

"DeFranco, right?"

She nodded and looked around the courthouse suspiciously. "I'm sorry, who are you?"

"Detective Shawn Johnson. I know we don't really know each other."

Rubbing her forehead, she was a bit embarrassed. "Ugh. Of course. I'm so sorry. What can I do for you, Detective?"

He moved closer to her and spoke quietly. "Brandon DeFranco has been a thorn in this department's side for as long as he has been writing for the Tribune. These charges need to stick."

"I'm not sure what it is I can do about that. Maybe you should be talking to Lydia?"

"You're the one Lydia will listen to."

"Well, if my victim still wants to follow through, that is who Lydia technically listens to."

"So, get your victim to listen to *you*." He grinned devilishly and winked before going back over to the police station.

Elizabeth shook the confusion from her face and walked through the large wooden doors on the opposite side of the hall, her eyes circled the courtroom until she saw Pam sitting with Brandon. *Awe shit*, she said to herself. She called out Pam's name and upon recognition and waved her hand motioning her to follow. Pam quietly spoke a few words to her husband before getting up from her seat and following Elizabeth into the hallway. The look on her face was pure shame.

Taking a deep breath as they sat on a bench just outside the courtroom, Elizabeth attempted to assess the situation. "Pam, how are you doing?"

Apprehensive, she tried to explain, "Well, as you can see, we're trying to work things out."

"I see that. But how are *you*?"

"I'm tired and I just want things to go back to normal."

"You know, I read through the evaluation you gave me. Things do not seem too normal."

Crossing her arms defensively she asked, "What do we need to do to make all this go away?"

She refrained from rolling her eyes. "This isn't just going to go away. Right now all I can do is tell the prosecutor where you stand. Brandon's attorney will take care of the rest. The prosecutor could give him a plea deal."

"A plea deal?"

"Yes. That means he could be offered a lesser offense to plead guilty to."

Sighing, she placed her elbows on her knees and buried her face in her hands.

Touching her forearm, Elizabeth tried to console her. "Look, this is typically what happens. At least he wouldn't have a domestic violence conviction on his record." She could tell her efforts were for naught. "Let me talk to the prosecutor and see what is going on, okay? Sit tight."

Making her way through the clerk's office, Elizabeth opened the door to the judge's chambers and took a seat in front of the desk across from Lydia who was thumbing through DeFranco's small file. She grabbed the police report, scanning it. "What do you have for me? Did you talk to your victim?"

"They're working it out, of course."

Lydia looked up at Elizabeth and smiled, "Of course. You know he doesn't have an attorney?"

"Really?" Remembering what Shawn asked of her, she decided to try and take one for the team. Setting the evaluation on the desk in front of Lydia, she said, "I think Pamela DeFranco gave me this for a reason."

Picking up the document, she reviewed the highlights. "Nice. But you know we can't use this?"

"What do you mean? His wife gave it to me. Obviously, she's concerned."

"It's confidential. His wife shouldn't even have it.

Come on, Liz, you should know that. Give it back to her. You can't keep that in your file."

She let out a frustrated sigh. "So what should I tell her?"

"I'm offering to drop the disruption of public service if he pleads to the misdemeanor domestic violence. At least if he's charged again with a DV it will be a felony but, I'm guessing this was a one-time-thing. He can go through anger management classes and be put on probation for the next six months. I'll meet with him while you talk to her and see how he wants to proceed."

"I doubt it was a one-time-thing, but I'll let Pam know. Thanks Lydia."

Elizabeth returned to the lobby and took a deep breath before sitting down next to Pam. She looked as tired as Elizabeth felt and it wasn't even time for lunch. "I just talked with Lydia, the prosecutor, and she's going to offer Brandon a plea deal. If he pleads guilty to the domestic violence charge, she will drop the other charges. Of course, this means he will need to complete anger management classes and be on probation for the next six months as well."

The expression on her face was a mixture of disbelief, anger, and confusion. "But – I'm not pursuing anything. I'm here in support of him. Didn't you tell her that?"

"Of course I did. I told her the two of you are working things out. She's well aware you are not interested in pursuing anything."

"Then why do they have it out for him so bad? You

know, his articles about the police department and the entire system in this town in general are important. His work *is* important."

Growing impatient, Elizabeth took a breath and tucked her hair behind her right ear in an attempt to calm her nerves. *I think it's time for a happy pill. This one is wearing off.* "Pam, no one has it out for your husband, but he certainly hasn't made any friends here. You have to remember, just because you changed your mind since your original call to the police, they still have a job to do. Every case is reviewed the same. Not every case has the same outcome. You are free to change your mind, but when it comes down to it, you mess with the bull, you get the horns. It's that simple."

A tear streamed down her cheek out of frustration as she bit the side of her lip to hold back her anger. Grabbing her purse beside her, she gracefully stood up. "I'm sorry, Elizabeth, but this is nothing but pure backlash for the important work my husband does. When all this began, you told me you would be here until I no longer wanted you to be."

Seriously lady? "And I stand by that," she said in an attempt not to show her own frustrations.

"Good. Because I no longer want you to be." With that she stormed off into the courtroom to be with her husband.

She stretched out her neck before paying Lydia a visit to fill her in. "It's all yours, Lydia. My work is done here," she said as she fanned her hands in the air. Lydia thanked her for her time and looked at her with sympathy. "Hey, Liz, good luck today. We're all thinking about you."

With a half grin, she nodded her head and walked into the clerk's office just outside the judge's chambers. Feeling a little embarrassed yet again she thought, *Does everyone know about this?* Taking another deep breath, she attempted to concentrate on herself for a moment rather than a victim in distress. She needed a drink of water and a pill. The lobby seemed quiet enough, but her heels made an unwelcome echo on the marble floors. Reaching in her bag, she pulled out the prescription bottle. Looking at it curiously, she wondered when she could just toss them in the trash.

Popping a Valium in her mouth, she washed it down with ice-cold water from the fountain and pulled her phone from the front pocket of her bag. She already had a text from Martinez, 'In the parking lot on the side, meet me out here when you're done.' She smiled and headed out to meet him.

As the handicap accessible door swung open upon her pressing the button, she saw Martinez standing next to his black Impala. He was dressed in a black T-shirt and dark jeans, the sun gleaming off of his badge, which was attached to his belt. He was a sight for tired, sore eyes. But it was surely a rough week for him as well. The little patch of hair under his bottom lip was blending with the remainder of his unshaven face and his grown out, military haircut. He smiled as she walked out the door and at that moment, it was all she could see. When she reached him, he wrapped his arms around her waist and greeted her, "Hola, bella."

Looking up at him she responded with a greeting of her own. "Hola, guapo."

His brown eyes shimmered with excitement. "Nice! Learning a little Spanish, are we?" She rolled her eyes flirtatiously. His expression became sober. "Are you ready for this?"

Pulling away from his embrace, she made her way to the passenger side of the vehicle and opened the door. "I am *not* ready for this. What I'm ready for is a warm bath and a nice glass of Chardonnay." Though she was happy to see him, the reason for their meeting kicked her back to reality.

Realizing how stupid his question sounded after the fact, he quietly retreated to his position in the driver's seat and started the engine. Elizabeth barely spoke during the entire trip to Mansfield and Martinez refused to force conversation. She stared out the window the entire time watching the curves of the white lines on the road sweetly embrace the rolling plains.

As they entered the Mansfield city limits, her heart began to race. It had only been an hour, but she felt as if the Valium she gulped down at the courthouse was wearing off, again. After a few more turns in the road, the prison was in view. Martinez took his eyes off the road for a moment and glanced at her. The tension grew the closer the vehicle came to the entrance. He reached over and grabbed her sweaty palm as a reassurance. She squeezed his hand, her eyes fixated on the barbed wire fence surrounding the compound while she practiced her breathing techniques.

Martinez flipped the turn signal and began to turn the vehicle onto the prison property. Elizabeth looked at the back of her eyelids and slowly took a deep breath, clinching his hand for dear life. "I don't think I can do this."

Pulling the vehicle off to the side, he placed it in park and turned to her. Peering into her eyes with the strength she was lacking, he promised, "I told you, I'm not leaving your side. He can't hurt you anymore, Liz."

With another deep breath she nodded her head, "Okay, let's do it."

Placing the car into drive, he continued on to the guard shack near the entrance where he was to meet Investigator McMurphy. He pulled up next to the window with his identification ready to give the gray haired guard. "How's it going?"

The man's eyes looked up over his wire-framed glasses while his hunting magazine rested on his belly and he replied in a gruff voice, "'Nother day 'nother dollar." He placed the magazine on his small desk, took a glance at Martinez's ID, and searched for his list of visitors.

"We're meeting Investigator McMurphy. Detective Angel Martinez and Elizabeth Strong."

Searching the list through his bifocals, the man shook his head back and forth. "Sorry, Detective, I don't have either of you."

"I'm afraid you may be mistaken. Could you have another look?"

"Look, Detective, I'm sorry. I-do-not-have-you."

Elizabeth and Martinez looked at each other with mutual shock. "Let's just go back," Elizabeth pleaded. "This is not a good sign."

Martinez turned back to the guard who was eagerly waiting to get back to his daily reading material. "Hey, I know you're just doing your job but this is *extremely* important. Investigator McMurphy is expecting us. Could you give him a ring and we can straighten this all out? Please?"

The guard looked at him again from beneath his glasses and pursed his lips. Without responding verbally, he picked up the phone, hit a number, and had a short conversation. "Go on through. Investigator McMurphy will meet you at the entrance to your left."

"Thank you! Have a wonderful day, Sir." He patted Elizabeth on the leg and found a parking spot past the guard shack. They exited the vehicle and walked towards McMurphy who was waiting for them at the door.

Martinez put out his right hand and gave a firm handshake as he spoke. "Investigator McMurphy, good to see you again. This is Elizabeth Strong."

Elizabeth reached out to shake his hand as well. "Investigator, nice to meet you. Thank you for setting this up with Detective Martinez, I do appreciate it."

"Detective, Miss Strong. I apologize but I'm confused as to why you're both here?"

Martinez looked perturbed. "Where is the confusion? I set this up with you weeks ago and sent in my confirmation Monday just as you asked."

Remaining calm, Investigator McMurphy said, "I never received that confirmation, Detective. Actually, I got word they were moving the hearing and I sent you an email with the new date and time. I assumed, since I still heard nothing, that Miss Strong here had changed her mind."

Elizabeth felt a small sense of relief while Martinez became agitated. He grabbed his chin and paced towards the car, then turned back around to McMurphy. "So you never received my confirmation?"

McMurphy shook his head, "Negative."

"I didn't receive your email, Investigator."

"I can only assume the email went through with no issue. I did not receive a Mailer-Daemon informing me otherwise."

He grew more agitated, his dark brown eyes turning a deep yellow gold. "So when was the hearing pushed back to?"

"I'm afraid the hearing was held yesterday afternoon, Detective. I'm very sorry. I wish there was more I could do."

Martinez bowed his chest and crossed his arms, cupping his unshaven face with his right hand. He took a deep breath before speaking. "I apologize for all the confusion, Investigator. I do appreciate you coming out here to let us know personally. We won't take up any more of your time."

After exchanging their goodbyes, Elizabeth and Martinez settled into the front seat of the Impala. "Damn it!" he yelled as he slammed his hand on the steering wheel, making Elizabeth jump. Her eyes scanned the perimeter; the steel doors, the guard shacks, the armed towers and the high fences with barbed wire. The pill she had taken earlier was definitely beginning to wear off.

"Can we please just get the hell out of here?"

He wiped the stress from his face with his hands and turned to her. "I'm so sorry, Liz. I messed up."

"This wasn't your fault. Why would you say something like that?"

"Actually, it is my fault. I depended on someone else to do my shit, to have my back." He started the engine to the car and put it in gear. "That'll be the last time."

During the trip back to Silverton, Martinez explained how he asked Johnson to handle the request for him and had no idea what happened. He was furious that he hadn't taken care of it himself or made the effort to try and confirm that the request had been sent and received. So much so, the entire hour long drive, he did nothing but continue to apologize. Finally pulling into the parking lot at the courthouse, Martinez parked next to Elizabeth's worn Beamer.

With both hands still on the steering wheel, he looked out the windshield in disgust. "I'm such an idiot." He looked over at her; she was gazing at him empathetically. "I'm sorry, Liz. Really, I am."

Tucking her hair behind her ear, she shook her head.

"Will you *please* stop saying that?" She took his hand from the wheel and held onto it. "Look, whatever happened, it happened. There's nothing we can do about it now and frankly, if you couldn't tell, I wasn't exactly thrilled about going in the first place."

"Yeah, well, Johnson has some explaining to do."

"Maybe he got busy and it slipped his mind. Maybe the Chief snagged him up right after you that day and sent him off on some other wild detective outing. I'm sure there's an explanation. Either way, it's done. I'm sure we'll know the results of the hearing soon enough. At least we got out of the office for the afternoon, right?" She smiled.

He squeezed her hand and smiled back, shaking his head. "You're amazing, you know that?"

"I'm amazingly exhausted. I gotta get back to the office and then I'm going home and have plans with a nice hot bath, some music, and some wine."

"Hmm, sounds like you might need some assistance," he said flexing his eyebrows flirtatiously.

"I think I got it covered. But it is tempting." *It is so tempting!*

Somewhat discouraged from being shot down, he understood. "Can I call you later?"

She leaned in closer to him for a kiss goodbye, "Of course."

CHAPTER 6

Dragging herself down the hallway to the office lobby, Elizabeth reached the front desk. Andrea glanced up at her from behind the bulletproof glass window and buzzed her in. It seemed like a quiet afternoon. Everyone was too busy in their offices to notice her entrance. She didn't much feel like explaining her ordeal anyway. Of course, she could never sneak past China. Today, she didn't even try. Holding onto her bag strapped across her torso, she reached China's office and leaned on the doorway. Feeling a presence, China spun around in her chair. She was pleasantly surprised.

"Hey! What are you doing back so soon? How did it go?"

Melting into the chair on the other side of China's desk, she sighed and rolled her eyes. "It didn't."

"What the hell is that supposed to mean?"

"It means it didn't go. We drove all the way there, I

swear I felt like I was going to vomit the entire drive, only to get there and find out the hearing was moved."

"Awe honey, I'm sorry. So, when did they move it to?"

"Yesterday," she said matter-of-factly.

"WHAT? I'm sorry, I don't think I heard you right."

"Apparently there was an issue with the request getting there and an email got lost, I don't know. Honestly, I don't really care at this point. I obviously wasn't meant to be there."

China was beyond irritated, her eyes appearing black behind the slits of her eyelids. "How the hell do you lose an email? I call bullshit." She looked at her watch; it was almost 2:30. "You wanna have a cigarette? You look like you could use a cigarette."

Leaning her head back and gazing at the ceiling, she thought for a moment. "What the hell. Then I think I'm going to take off and go home. I have some personal time and I'm over it."

They both rose from their seats and started down the hall to let the secretaries know they were taking a break. Before they could reach the door, Peggy called out to them from her office.

"Elizabeth?"

They both stopped just past the opening of Peggy's office door and China whispered an expletive. Elizabeth took a couple steps back, her eyes locked with China's as she lipped 'Oh my God!' She turned away and poked her head in Peggy's office. "Yes, Peggy?"

"I need to speak with you. Have a seat, please."

Turning back to China for a moment she rolled her eyes out of Peggy's view.

"Cankles," whispered China.

Elizabeth held in a laugh and shook her head before stepping into the dragon's lair. Peggy sat at her desk with amazing posture and looked down her nose at Elizabeth. She wasn't an ugly woman. She had a smaller waistline and fuller in her bum and legs with shoulder length, bottle blonde hair, but her snobbish demeanor was off putting and made her less desirable.

"So you had the pretrial for Brandon DeFranco today?"

"Yes," said Elizabeth as she nodded her head.

"Well, I'm afraid we have an issue but I wanted to get your side before I took this to Marilyn." She moved the mouse on her keyboard to wake up her computer screen.

My side? What the hell is she talking about? Elizabeth realized Peggy was on the website for the Silverton Tribune. Brandon DeFranco had a busy afternoon. The entire conversation she had with Pam at the pretrial was now online for the world, or at least the entire city of Silverton, to read. *What the fu...*

Peggy scrolled down to a line that was highlighted. "I need to know if this is what you said to Mrs. DeFranco."

In her fury, Elizabeth read the passage:

'VICTIM ADVOCATE, Elizabeth Strong, did not hold back when asked why SPD and the prosecutor didn't seem as if they wanted to work with a first time offender. She specifically said, "When you mess with the bull, you get the horns.'"

Shocked and humiliated, her mouth agape, Elizabeth didn't know how to respond to the question. She felt betrayed while she silently searched for a way to best word her response. "Peggy, I – I don't know what to say." She sighed in discomfort.

"Right now, you just need to answer the question I asked you. Did you say this to Mrs. DeFranco?"

Her heart began to beat a little faster and the look on her face became defensive. "No – well, yes – but – it wasn't like that. This is totally being taken out of context!"

Peggy cocked her head and spoke through her nose with more authority. "When it's written down and then read, there is no other context but what the writer wants there to be. The article, as written, makes it appear that SPD and the prosecutor's office has it out for Brandon DeFranco due to his past articles about us and he uses your words to verify it. This isn't good, Elizabeth."

Elizabeth opened her mouth to speak and stopped herself. She sat back in the chair and shook her head, frustrated. With Peggy's demeanor and tone, she was seemingly uninterested in hearing Elizabeth's defense. "I don't know what else you want me to say, Peggy. I said that to mean the same thing as 'don't do the crime if you can't do the time.' I can't help the context in which he wrote it."

"I'll talk with Marilyn about this but for now, I think

it's best if you just go home for the day. In our positions, we need to be real careful about what we say and how we say it."

Not holding back on her feelings of amusement, and frustration, Elizabeth rolled her eyes and shook her head slightly as she laughed out of her nose. "You know, Peggy, I was planning on going home anyway, but thanks for your concern." She stood up abruptly and stomped out of the office. *Who in the hell does she think she is?*

Briskly skipping down the stairwell, Elizabeth was fuming, hoping China was still outside taking her break. She took the parking garage elevator to the top level. When the doors opened she stepped outside to find China still smoking and on her cell phone. Her face lit up with relief.

"I gotta go, I'll call ya later," China said before ending her call. "Hey, Liz, what the hell was that all about?"

"Can I please bum a cigarette?"

Reaching in her pack and pulling out a Misty Menthol, she handed it to Elizabeth with her lighter. She looked at her sympathetically and asked, "What happened?"

The flame burned the tobacco and she inhaled the carcinogenic fumes along with the nicotine, instantly relaxing her nerves. Slowly exhaling, she closed her eyes and propelled her face towards the sun. When she opened her eyes, she looked at China. "I'm not gonna make it. I swear to God, anything that could have gone wrong today, did!"

After filling China in on the details, she was almost as

pissed off as Elizabeth. "What a bitch! Liz, don't even sweat that shit. You should have went straight to Marilyn's office and explained yourself."

"China, I just honestly don't feel like dealing with this shit today. First of all, I can't believe I let Angel talk me into going to Mansfield. That was a frigin' disaster! Then, Pam totally throws me under the bus. And now, Peggy has the nerve to be all high and mighty. Her confidence is rather annoying." She took another long drag of her cigarette.

China held out her French manicured hand as a signal to stop Elizabeth's ranting. "Okay, let's put all this in perspective, shall we? Angel is a Godsend. No pun intended – well, maybe a little." She laughed. Elizabeth wasn't amused. "Okay, seriously, so things got a little mixed up with the hearing. Big deal. Like you said, you didn't wanna go anyway, right? No harm, no foul."

Giving her a look like she knew she was right, Elizabeth rolled her eyes and shook her head in agreement.

"Okay. Second, Brandon DeFranco is a journalist for the Silverton Tribune who literally gets a hard on for a story like this! Did you expect anything less from his own wife?" China glared at her as if she was waiting for her to disagree so she could slap her back into reality and take great pleasure in it.

Although she knew she was right, she was dead on actually, Elizabeth still felt betrayed. Here she was, wasting her energy and her time, for a woman who had obviously been gaslighted. Just another victim she couldn't reach.

"And as for Peggy? Screw her! Sitting up there on her Ivory Tower. Confidence? I'm sorry but you can't have the confidence of a runway model and look like a doctor's wife." She lit another cigarette out of frustration.

Elizabeth giggled. "What the hell is that supposed to mean?"

A tad irritated she had to explain herself, she happily informed her friend. "It means she's homely, Liz. She's confident she has the doctor because she has the three-carat diamond on her finger, but she doesn't really have him. The twenty-four-year-old nurse he's banging in the broom closet on his break while they're both snorting Ritalin in between patients, has him." Her Asian eyes widened as she pursed her lips as if to say, 'Duh.'

Elizabeth's face showed a bit of surprise. She shook her head and smiled shamefully.

"Tell me I'm wrong."

HAVING an hour to stew over what happened to his request, Martinez glided up the stairs to the detective bureau like an angry deity. His face was red by the time he reached the office, sweat beading on his forehead. Shawn was sitting at his desk, deep in thought about whatever he was reading on his computer. He glanced up upon Martinez's hard footsteps coming towards him. Shawn backed up in his chair a bit and began to stand, nearly expecting a backlash of sorts.

Martinez swiftly gained traction and headed straight for Shawn's throat with his hands. The two men fell back onto the wall, Martinez yelling the entire time. "You son of a bitch! You knew how important this was! I thought you had my back!" His grip grew stronger.

Choking on his words, Shawn attempted to explain himself. "Martinez! What the hell?"

Chief Holden heard the commotion and quietly made his presence known within the room filled with testosterone. He leaned against the doorway and crossed his long arms across his chest, calmly but clamorously asking, "What the hell is going on here?"

Martinez released Shawn's throat and shoved him in the chest, his back making a loud thud against the wall behind him. The fury in his eyes remained as he glared at his colleague. "Well, I don't know, Chief. Why don't you ask Johnson why my request never made it to Mansfield and Liz missed the parole hearing!"

Removing his glasses from his tired face, he wiped them clean with the handkerchief from his shirt pocket before adjusting them back on his nose. "This true, Johnson?"

Befuddled, Shawn grasped for words. "Chief, I have no idea what he's talking about. One minute I'm sitting here working, the next, he's literally at my damn throat!"

Not able to contain himself, Martinez continued to yell. "Chief, I asked him to send in my request to Investigator McMurphy. McMurphy said he never received it. Johnson said he sent it!"

Holden remained calm. Looking at Martinez from over the top of his glasses, his eyes expressed a warning. "I think you're going to need to take it down a decibel or two."

Martinez took a deep breath and exhaled slowly before he continued. "McMurphy also said he emailed me the change in the hearing but I never received it. We arrived there today, only to find out the hearing was held yesterday!"

For a moment, Holden gazed at Martinez, not looking into his eyes, but through them. Then he moved on to Shawn who was waiting for his turn with a piece of paper in his hands. "What do you have to say about this, Johnson?"

Handing the sheet of paper to him, he defended himself. "This is the email I sent in on Monday." He turned to Martinez, "Look, man, obviously I did screw up without even realizing. After you left, Chief needed me to go check out another OD. I mistakenly sent the email to general requests at Mansfield instead of directly to McMurphy, not even thinking about it. Still, it should have gotten to him. I'm sorry, man."

"Johnson, you knew how important this was and why didn't I get McMurphy's email? That doesn't make any sense."

"Really Martinez? I don't mean to be a dick but if it was so important why didn't you send the damn thing yourself? And how is it my fault or my problem that you didn't get *his* email?"

The look on his face was a cross between appalled and stupefied. "Are you freaking kidding me, Johnson?"

Before Martinez had the chance to go after Shawn's throat again, Holden took control of the room. "Johnson, don't you have somewhere to be right now?"

Pushing his chair under his desk with force, Shawn exited the room. Holden looked at Martinez and sympathized logically. "I'm sorry Elizabeth missed her hearing. You know these things sometimes happen, Martinez. Wires get crossed. Not sure what happened to the email *from* Mansfield to you but you may want to ask McMurphy about that before you go pointing fingers."

Sighing in disgust, Martinez knew the Chief was right. "How'd Elizabeth take it?"

Raising his head and shaking it proudly, he threaded his arms across his chest. "She doesn't seem to care much. Not that she doesn't care, I just - I know she's scared."

Holden nodded, "Rightfully so. I understand you have strong feelings for her but I told you from the get-go to tread lightly on this. Don't let yourself care more about it than she does and don't push her too hard." Turning his tall, lanky frame around to return to his office he looked at Martinez one last time before adding, "And Johnson's a good detective. Take it easy."

ON HER SECOND glass of Chardonnay, the warm lake breeze and the setting sun were finally bringing Elizabeth some peace to her stressful day. She took one more sip of wine, set the glass on the wicker table in front of her, and ventured into the bathroom to fill the tub. "Lavender, for balance," she said aloud, remembering her mother's advice as she sat on the side of the tub, allowing a few drops of oil to mix with the swirling hot water.

Leaving the tub to fill, she sat down on the living room floor and thumbed through the album collection to find the best one with lyrics able to reflect her mood. *Pink Floyd, Wish You Were Here, 1975. Perfect.* Though neither of her parents suffered a breakdown like Syd Barrett, they were no longer with her and they weren't coming back.

"Shine on You Crazy Diamond" began echoing throughout the house. Returning to the bath, she shut off the water. The old claw foot bathtub had reached its limit. She lit some candles and conveniently placed her wine glass next to them on the built-in shelf surrounding the tub before stripping down to her birthday suit. The door remained open so she could hear the music and allowed the room to remain cool enough against the steam.

Slipping into the water, it was as hot as her bare skin could endure. She sunk until the water reached the nape of her neck, covering all other extremities, closed her eyes and took a deep breath. As she exhaled, "Wish You Were Here" began to play. Singing along, tears began to form at the crease in her eyelids. She thought of her parents. What would they do right now? What would they say to her to make this terrible day seem like a distant nightmare? *You're Strong, Elizabeth...* Her father's voice echoed in her head.

She didn't feel strong. She felt like getting dressed and packing a bag, cleaning out her trust account, and disappearing. For good. Forgetting about the small town she was from and everyone in it. *I could sign over the title of the lake house to Bill and Marta for their troubles; they would understand. China's a grown woman; she doesn't need me for anything. And Martinez – he could –* Grappling for an easy way out, she told herself, *- he doesn't need me adding any more drama to his life than I already have.*

Frustrated with her own thoughts, she dunked the washcloth in the water and slapped it on her face, the water mixing with her tears. After wiping away the need to feel sorry for herself, she tried to pull it together like she knew her parents would want her to do. *What if he does get out early? He really doesn't give a shit about a protection order, so why bother? But I do need to be prepared...* She closed her eyes again and inhaled the lavender that stimulated the air.

Pink Floyd continued to play as the multiple record turntable worked its magic, until there was a loud banging on the dining room door. "You have got to be kidding me!" Elizabeth stood in the tub, the water rushing back and forth from the force of her body. She grabbed her towel from the stool beside her. There was impatient banging on the door again. "Just a minute," she tried to yell over the music. She pushed the bathroom door shut, just in case she was in view.

Throwing on her terry cloth robe, she went to the door, peeking through the blinds before unlatching the lock. It was Martinez. She smiled and turned the deadbolt to the left. "Hey you! I thought you were going to call?"

He stepped into the dining room and tossed his keys onto the table. "I've been trying to call. I was worried about you." He grabbed her, pulling her close to him. His voice was distantly monotone. "I see I caught you at the perfect time." He kissed her hard on her lips, scratching her face with his stubble.

Attempting to back away, she was put off by his aggressiveness. "What's gotten into you?"

"When you didn't answer, I was beginning to think you were avoiding me." He tightened his grip on her waist. "You wouldn't avoid me now, would you, Lizzy?"

Her heart sunk deep within her chest before she slapped him across the face. Her eyes deepened with confusion as his face turned red with fury before he threw her up against the wall with one swift motion of his right hand around her throat. She couldn't scream. Her mouth was gasping for air that wouldn't come, like a fish in the hot sun that just washed up on the sand. Tears welled in her eyes and trickled down her face from the compounding fear and the inability to breath.

He tilted his head, his face stone cold as she struggled. "Isn't this how you like it, Lizzy?"

There was a knock at the door and his hand fell to his

side releasing her. She sucked the air desperately making a sickly sound as she placed her own hands around her throat as if to help the air enter her body. Upon the water entering her windpipe, Elizabeth's eyes shot open and she grabbed the sides of the tub and forced herself to sit up, the water slashing around her. She grabbed the towel beside her on the stool and shoved it to her face as her lungs expelled the small amount of liquid that choked her. There was another knock at the door.

Becoming concerned, Martinez rapped at the door impatiently over the music. "Liz? Are you okay?" He paced back and forth across the wooden floor on the porch periodically looking in the windows and wondering how long he should wait before kicking the door in. He leaned his elbow on the wall beside the door and grabbed his forehead, then he heard the deadbolt unlock.

The door slowly opened and Elizabeth stood there, her body drenched beneath her robe. Staring into space, her demeanor seemed bewildered and begged for solace. Her eyes slowly moved towards his as her hand remained on the doorknob. She didn't move. He opened the screen door and walked in.

"Liz? What's wrong?" he asked softly.

A tear fell from the corner of her eye. She didn't speak. As he went to touch her shoulder, her body jerked in fear. He rested his hand on her upper arm. "Hey, it's me. It's okay."

As her bottom lip began to quiver, it was as if the levy had broken. Tears streamed down her face and her nostrils shut off all air to them while the nightmare replayed in her head. He pulled her close and held her tight allowing her a slight release. Once she let out a good cry, she pulled away wiping her eyes ashamedly. "I'm sorry," she said before turning away to the bathroom so she could clear her airways and wipe her face. She couldn't bear to share it with him.

Martinez was waiting for her on the couch. Sitting down next to him, she tucked a loose lock of hair behind her ear. "I'm sorry."

"Liz, you have nothing to be sorry for. I'm sorry for dragging you down to Mansfield for nothing."

She shook her head. "It's not just that. You were right about DeFranco. No sooner had we returned, he had a nice write up in the Tribune."

He sighed and looked at her sympathetically but his eyes said, 'I told you so.'

"Worst part is, Pam saw the 'article' and was going to Marilyn, like I did something wrong!" Telling him about how the rest of her day played out made it much easier to forget her dream. All she wanted to do was forget it. It was typical to dream about Steve hurting her, expected even. But putting Martinez in Steve's shoes was on a whole other level.

"I'm sorry you had such a bad day. If it's any consolation, mine wasn't the greatest either," he told her, recalling his falling out with Johnson. Although he debated whether or not he should share, he decided it was best to leave this to himself and see how it played out.

Already beginning to feel better she said, "I'm going to put some clothes on. Would you like something to drink?"

He smiled. "You gotta beer?"

Smiling back at him, she raised herself from the sofa and went to her bedroom to put on a loose white T-shirt and a pair of pink boxer shorts. He heard her clanging around in the kitchen before returning to the living room with a Corona and a glass of wine in either hand. Standing in front of him and handing him his beer, she said, "Come here. I want to show you something." Her head tilted to the side asking him to follow her.

Taking his beer from her hand, he stood up and walked behind her to the back of the sofa. There was a door on the back wall just between the hanging mirror next to the staircase and the wall before the dining room. He always assumed it was a closet. Elizabeth looked at him and took a deep breath. Upon opening the door, it was just as Martinez imagined; a small storage space containing coats hanging on a rod extended from one end to the other and shoes and boxes and other miscellaneous items were strewn on the floor. Everything you would expect to be in a closet.

Standing in front of the doorway, Martinez took a sip of his beer and nodded his head. He wasn't sure what to say or what she was showing him but he patiently entertained her. She stood there for a moment, as if to catch her bearings for some unexpected C.S. Lewis plot to unfold before them. Cupping a stack of hangers with both hands, she pushed them to either side of the rod and then moved a flat piece of wood panel revealing another, somewhat smaller, door. The expression on his face changed. He was now intrigued.

She turned the doorknob and pushed open the door as she flipped on the light switch on the closet wall. Walking through the door, she took a step down into the room. Turning to him, she said, "Watch your step."

He followed her, careful not to trip over the two steps going down. His eyes scanned the room in awe. The walls and the floor were whitewashed wood with paintings artistically hung. There was a large easel placed near the corner of the room with a canvas nestling in its sleeve and covered with a white cloth. Shelves of different paints, brushes, and tiny tools he couldn't identify hung on the wall to the side of the easel. A metal stool sat in front of it, facing a covered window, with a paint-splattered smock hanging over the seat. There were paintings sitting against the walls and propped up on the legs of a busy desk that hadn't been dusted in years. Several unique sculptures and other artwork was scattered pleasantly throughout the room.

"Wow. What is all this?" He turned to her questionably. "Don't tell me you're an artist too?"

She took a sip of her wine and sighed. "Yeah, I wish." Looking at him with a sense of bitter sweetness, she grinned. "This was my mom's studio. I haven't been in here since the accident. I used to love coming in here when my mom was working."

Impressed, he asked, "She did this for a living?"

"Yeah, for quite a while. She was an art teacher for years but once my dad made partner at the firm, she started painting what inspired her. She did okay with it, she wasn't a famous artist or anything." She tilted her head and smiled at the memories. "It was a nice little part-time business though."

"You're mom seems like she was a pretty interesting individual."

"She was. She was amazing. I wish I were more like her. I'm afraid I took after my dad being analytical, suspicious, and logical. Or shall I say, boring?"

Grabbing her by the small of her back his strong hands wrapped around her waist. "You are far from boring, Elizabeth Strong." He pulled her a little closer. "And at least you know which parent's character traits you've inherited. The jury's still out on me."

Cupping his cheek with the palm of her hand, she gently swiped his full bottom lip. "I imagine you're a lot like your mom, Angel Martinez." Or rather she hoped.

artinez woke to the sound of his phone vibrating against the coffee table. He was just able to reach it without disturbing Elizabeth who was nestled under the throw blanket and half on top of him. They had fallen asleep comfortably on the sofa. The time on his phone read 6:57 am. Clearing his throat as quietly as he could, he answered. "Martinez."

"Martinez, it's Lacy. Chief wants you down at the public boat launch. We've gotta live one."

"Shit."

"Don't kill the messenger, alright? There are already a couple cruisers down there. Coroner should be there not long after you arrive."

"Sorry, Lacy. Not really how I wanted to start my weekend. Gimme twenty?" Upon confirmation, he placed the phone back on the table.

Elizabeth looked up at him with sleepy eyes from her comfortable pillow made from his pec. "Who was that?"

He kissed her forehead and held her close. "Can we just run away? Somewhere far from here?"

Nestling her face in his chest, she moaned. Then she threw the blanket on the back of the couch and made herself get up from the warmth of his body. She stood in front of him as he gazed at her tenderly. "Let me make you some coffee to take with you," she said before turning from him and heading to the kitchen.

He quickly rose from his overnight makeshift bed and began gathering his things. "Liz, I really appreciate it, but I don't have time. I have to get into town. They found a body down by the docks."

She looked at him and curiously raised her eyebrows. "Well, I guess they're not going anywhere are they?"

Amused he said, "Okay, can I take a to-go cup?"

She smiled. "Of course."

Martinez drove into town sipping his coffee along the way. Coming close to downtown, he turned left onto Shelby Street and drove two blocks to the boat docks. Next door, a cargo ship was pouring salt onto a mound getting ready for the winter season to come. One cruiser was blocking the entrance to the parking lot and backed up to allow Martinez entry. He pulled around and parked next to the other two cruisers and a truck from the fire department. It was early and already humid, the smell of fish staining the heavy air.

Officer Lucas walked up to meet Martinez at the edge of the embankment. "Good morning, Detective."

Looking over Lucas' shoulder he responded, "Morning, Lucas. What do we got so far?"

Lucas shook his head and scratched behind his ear. "Well, Duval is talking to the jogger over there who found the body and called it in." He pointed over to Officer Duval and a young lady in running clothes sitting on the park bench overlooking the lake. "And the fire department just got here. Two guys suited up and they're pulling her out now. So far, it looks like a female anyway. Coroner should be on the way."

Before Martinez could ask anything else, they heard a vehicle pulling in. The coroner's van backed up to the sidewalk close to them and parked. Dr. Wexler, a petite fellow, hopped out of the passenger side of the van. Sweat beads were already forming on the top of his bald head, which was surrounded by a half moon of graying, brown hair. His assistant left the drivers seat and joined him behind the van, opening the back doors to retrieve the gurney.

The firefighters lifted the body up onto the dock and laid it on its back. Dr. Wexler and Martinez walked down the wooden strip to the corpse, his assistant following behind with the gurney. "How have you been, Dr. Wexler?" asked Martinez.

His voice matched his small size. "Much better than our cadaver, I'm afraid. You're looking well, Detective."

Martinez picked up on the sarcasm. He was disheveled and he was well aware of it. He hadn't shaven in a week and he had been wearing the same clothes for the past two days. "I thank you for your dishonesty, Doctor."

As they reached the body, the firefighters stood to greet them. "Here you go fellas. She appears to have risen up just under the dock. Looks like her sundress got caught on the mollusks underneath. Good thing, otherwise the current could have washed her straight through the channel."

"Hey, Sizemore, thanks for doing our dirty work again." Martinez winked.

"No problem, man. We all know *real* men do dirty work."

Shaking his head he grinned. "And all this time I thought they carried guns."

Kenneth Sizemore was a big man with an even bigger heart. "Hey, you'll be at the spaghetti dinner next week, right?" he asked speaking of the fundraiser for his wife who was just diagnosed with breast cancer.

"Of course! I bought an extra ticket. Bringing a friend."

Walking back up the dock, Sizemore grinned and pointed at Martinez as if to say, 'You the man!'

Kneeling over the corpse, the two men placed latex gloves on their hands and Dr. Wexler began his examination. "Female in her mid to late 20's. Epidermis is wrinkled with pronounced discolorations; blanching and bloating appear to be underway." He gently pulled the drenched hair from her face and turned her chin towards him. "Initial estimations of cause of death point to drowning, however, there is an approximate three inch laceration from the frontal bone to the temporal bone indicating a possible point of impact caused by blunt force trauma."

The gut of the body appeared to be contracting. It began to spasm and its mouth and nose gurgled. Before Dr. Wexler could move out of the way, the corpse spewed a pinkish, red substance from its dead lips onto the lenses of his glasses. Martinez's face coiled as he covered his mouth, placing his forefinger under his nose so he could smell latex instead. It didn't help.

Dr. Wexler pulled off his glasses, wiped his face with a medicated hanky, leaned over and dunked his specs in the lake. Drying off the lenses he continued, "Putrefaction has begun as evidenced by the purge fluid that was just expelled." He examined her hands one by one. As he lifted her left hand, he looked up at Martinez. "Well, she's married. Someone has to be looking for her."

"Maybe. Then again, maybe they already know where she is." He wrapped his fingers around the charm in the shape of a heart hanging from a silver chain around her stiff, cold neck. It had a single diamond in the center surrounded by a starburst. Turning it around, there was an engraving on the back that read, *Love, Brandon.* "Shit."

"What is it, detective?"

"I think I just identified our victim."

"Ah. That is a good thing, yes?"

"Depends who you're asking."

"Of course. That sounds more like your line of expertise. For now, I am going to place the time of death somewhere within the past 24 hours. I'm afraid I won't know more until we perform the autopsy, which we need to conduct as soon as possible due to the circumstances. Once the body hits the air after being in the water for some time, the rate of decomposition is quite rapid."

Martinez stood up and said, "I understand, Doctor. Can you leave everything in tact until the ID is made? I can be there within the hour with a presumed family member."

"We have a few hours at least."

He nodded at Dr. Wexler's assistant and looked back to the doctor and said, "Okay, well, I'll leave you to it."

The doctor and his assistant prepared the body for transport as Martinez walked back up the dock to the sidewalk to meet Officer Lucas who was waiting for him.

"Lucas, make sure this entire area is sealed off. Take a look around and look for any signs of blood, a weapon, or personal belongings that might have been ditched. Have Duval check with the border patrol and find out if anyone was on duty at this port within the last 24 hours. Also, find out who owns that Buick over there. It looks out of place." Martinez pointed to an old four door, tan Buick with rust around the frame, which was parked in the middle of the parking lot. He grabbed his keys from his pocket and walked towards his vehicle.

Lucas looked irritated being left with the grunt work yet again. "Where are you going, Martinez?"

Leaning on the driver's side of his vehicle with the door open he hesitated for a moment. "I'm gonna try and ID our victim, Lucas. Once I do that, I have some very bad news to break to a few people. Unless, of course, you wanna trade?"

He immediately regretted asking the question. "I think I'll just stay here with Duval and investigate further."

"Good choice, Lucas."

DRIVING A FEW BLOCKS INTO DOWNTOWN, Martinez pulled into one of the diagonal spaces in front of the Silverton Tribune just in time for them to open at 8:00 am. It was a massive, old, three story stone building taking up the entire corner of Jackson Street and Water Street. *Tribune* was plastered on either side of the building in large letters. He entered the lobby through the front doors nestled within the large archway in the middle of the structure.

Making his way to the front counter, he was greeted by a young lady with shoulder length white hair and a bull piercing through the center of her nose. She wore a faded, black T-shirt with *I know my First Amendment rights* written on it and a closed fist underneath. Her blue eyes thrust beneath the dark liner on her lids. "How can I help you?" she asked.

Placing his hands on the counter, Martinez scoped out the place. "How's it going? I need to speak with Brandon DeFranco. Is he around?"

"He might be. Who are you?"

Flashing his badge on his belt he replied, "Detective Angel Martinez. It's official business. I'm afraid it's a private matter."

Looking at his badge then to his face, she said, "Yeah. Sure. Let me see if he's here." She came around the counter and headed up the wide marble staircase, disappearing into an office on the next floor. Within minutes she returned to her station behind the counter. "You can go on up. He's in the conference room across from the landing."

Martinez looked up the stairs. It was wide-open leading to the second floor. Nodding a thank you to the girl, he began up the staircase, holding onto the antique wooden rail. Reaching the landing, he glanced through the windows of the conference room. Brandon sat at a long table with two other people. The door was ajar, waiting for Martinez to enter. Rapping on the glass window of the door, he slowly entered the room.

An average sized man with blonde, spiky hair and icy blue eyes immediately stood to greet him, shoving his hand towards Martinez as an invitation. "Detective, come in, come in! We've much to discuss." He grabbed

Martinez's hand and shook it hard. "Jim West, managing editor of the Tribune. So glad to meet you."

"Nice to meet you Mr. West. I'm afraid I need to speak with Mr. DeFranco alone." Turning to Brandon he asked, "Is there somewhere we can speak in private?"

Before Brandon could answer, Jim spoke up again. "Nonsense, Detective. We've actually been hoping to have the chance to speak with you!"

Turning again to Brandon, Martinez said, "Mr. DeFranco, I'm afraid this is a delicate matter. You may want to consider some privacy."

Finally speaking for himself, Brandon closed the screen on his laptop and said, "It's okay, Detective. Anything you have to say to me can be said in front of my colleagues. I don't have anything to hide." The look on his young face seemed smug.

Sitting down on the other side of the conference table, Jim extended his arm to the seat on the end of the table offering it to Martinez. "Please, sit." He sat back in his chair and smiled, crossing his legs and resting his hands comfortably on top of his knees. "Would you like something to drink, Detective?" He turned to the pretty girl sitting next to him. "Sam, get the detective a water would you? And make sure this is recorded, would you please?"

"When was the last time you spoke with your wife, Mr. DeFranco?"

Sam set a water bottle down in front of Martinez and sat down next to Jim. She set the voice recorder on her phone, placed it in the middle of the table, and glanced at

Brandon. Catching his eyes for a moment, she gave him half a smile.

Rolling his eyes thinking for a moment, Brandon recalled, "Sometime yesterday. We were in court yesterday morning." Remembering the night of his arrest he said, "You're aware we had some problems."

Shaking his head affirmatively, Martinez replied, "I'm aware. So, you haven't talked to your wife since court yesterday?"

He nervously adjusted the collar of his polo. "I came into the office after that and worked late. Um, she sent me a text around 8:30, said she was staying at her sister's house."

"That was the last time you heard from your wife?"

"Well, yes. She needed some space. There's nothing illegal about that."

"Do you remember what your wife was wearing?"

Chiming in, Jim was less amused and more worried where the line of questioning was headed. "Where are you going with this, Detective? What is this all about?"

Acting as if he didn't hear him, Martinez asked the question again. "Do you remember what your wife was wearing yesterday, Mr. DeFranco?"

Brandon scratched his forehead and ran his fingers through his wavy brown hair. "I don't know – uh, a blue sundress? I'm with Jim. What exactly is going on here?"

"Mr. DeFranco, does your wife wear a heart pendant with a diamond sunburst and an engraving on the back?"

The chair made an unpleasant noise against the floor

as Brandon pushed back and rose from it. "How do you know that?" He placed one hand on his hip and the other on his chin. He looked at Jim then at Sam begging for an explanation. "How does he know that?"

Martinez stood and met Brandon's eyes. "I'm very sorry to be the one to tell you this, Mr. DeFranco but I believe we found your wife's body this morning."

Shock carried over him taking his speech and his breath. His body slumped back into his chair. "What the hell are you talking about?" He looked at Jim. "What the *hell* is he *talking* about, Jim?"

Jim was just as shocked. "Oh my. Are you sure, Detective? Pam?" he asked shaking his head.

Nodding his head, he turned back to Brandon. "Of course, I'll need you to come with me to the morgue to officially identify the body but I'm pretty confident it's Mrs. DeFranco." He put his head down for a moment, almost ashamed of his next question. "I'm sorry to have to ask you this, Mr. DeFranco, but can you tell me your whereabouts yesterday?"

A dumbfounded glare washed over his face. "Are you kidding me?" He turned to Jim. "Is he freaking kidding me?" Nestling his temples between his thumb and his middle finger, he massaged them before moving in and rubbing his eyes.

Sam jumped up from her seat and placed her hands on the table exclaiming, "He was with me." She was as surprised at her outburst as Brandon and Jim.

Finally, Jim stood from his seat. "Okay, I think we're

going to stop at this point in time. I'm sorry, Detective Martinez, but Brandon is going to need some time to process all this."

"Well I'm sorry Mr. West, I need him to identify the body."

"And I will take him to do that. Brandon, don't say another word. Detective, we'll meet you at the coroner," he said as he grabbed the door handle and nodded for Martinez to exit.

Pausing, Martinez stressed, "It will need to be done now. Request of the coroner due to time constraints, of course." As Martinez walked out the door, Jim assured him of their attendance and shut the door behind him.

"Christ, Brandon. I'm so sorry."

Samantha took to his side and placed her hand on his shoulder. "We don't know for sure it's her. Do you want me to come with you?"

Brandon pulled away, his tanned face turned pale and he needed hydration. He walked over to the water cooler unable to answer her.

Whispering, Jim said, "Sam, I know you're trying to help but I'm going to need you here. If it *is* Pam, I need you to take hold of his assignments and make sure our deadlines are met. He's certainly going to need it if his wife is laying up there at the morgue."

Sam sighed and rolled her eyes underneath her Betty Paige bangs. "I want to be there for him, Jim."

Gently placing his hand on her upper arm in a fatherly manner he assured her, "You will be. That would be a huge help to both Brandon *and* the Tribune. Right now, *I* need to help him with Detective Martinez. While we're taking care of this, get a hold of our legal department. Looks as if we're going to need them."

She opened the door to return to her office down the hall, glancing at Brandon with concern on her way out. "Please let me know as soon as you know something," she asked.

"Of course. And Sam, keep this under wraps. I don't want any leaks of any kind. When the time is right, we'll break the story properly and in our favor."

She shook her head as if she understood and left the two men to attend to their business.

When Jim and Brandon arrived at the coroner's office, Martinez was waiting for them on a bench just outside an examination room with a large glass window. Standing up to greet them, he said, "Thanks for coming down so quickly. Dr. Wexler is just prepping for the autopsy, so I'm afraid we won't be able to go in. Take you're time. Just let me know when you're ready."

Brandon stared at the cold steel table horizontally in line with the window, which held a figure covered by a light blue cloth. He watched Dr. Wexler and his assistant prepare their tools that would soon slice into the skin of someone who could be his wife. The thought alone made him turn away from the scene. Jim turned to his side. "I know this has to be excruciating, Brandon, but you have to do this. I'm so sorry."

Wiping his eyes and taking a deep breath, he turned back around to face the possible agony that awaited him. He nodded his head and took a deep breath again. Turning to Martinez he said, "Can we get this over with, please?"

Martinez tapped on the window and gave Dr. Wexler a head nod signaling they were ready. The doctor moved to the opposite side of the table, grabbed the edge of the cloth, and pulled it down to the waistline of the water-logged corpse. Letting out a breath of despair, Brandon bit his bottom lip to keep from whimpering. Jim rested his hand on Brandon's shoulder with no words to follow.

"Is that your wife, Mr. DeFranco?" asked Martinez.

Unable to answer, Brandon fell to the bench and placed his face into shaking hands. "This can't be happening," he cried. His breathing became heavy. He stood up, his face soaked with tears, and stormed down the hall forcefully pushing the swinging doors open to find an exit, desperate for fresh air.

Jim stood there with one arm across his chest while covering his mouth with his other hand, his eyes wide in disbelief. After a moment of silence, he spoke. "This is absolutely crazy. What the hell happened?"

Taking Brandon's actions and Jim's words as a positive ID, Martinez nodded again to the doctor who then ordered his assistant to pull down the shades. "Well, Mr. West, that's what I'm hoping to find out. We should have a few more answers after the autopsy is finished. You do know I'm going to need to speak with Mr. DeFranco again very soon. Preferably sometime this afternoon."

"Come on, Detective, the man just lost his wife. He has arrangements to make, people to notify, time to grieve, maybe? This can't be new to you."

"Well, no it's not but I'm sure you're aware the first 48 hours of a murder investigation are the most important."

His eyes lit up. "So, you're admitting this is a murder investigation?"

"I'm not confirming or denying that until we hear what Dr. Wexler has to say in his report but his wife was just found floating in Lake Erie. It's not as if she died of natural causes. It's suspicious and the initial findings currently support foul play. He's going to have to answer some questions here."

Jim nervously looked at the fancy watch on his wrist. "Look, it's almost 10 o'clock. I'm going to take him wher-ever he wants to go. I have no doubt you will have his full cooperation. Whatever you need, but can we give this until later this afternoon? I'm sure Brandon wants to figure out what happened as much as you do. How about we let this all sink in first and let him take care of a few things?"

Nodding in agreement, Martinez said, "Of course. I have some things to take care of myself." He handed Jim one of his cards. "Please have him call me this afternoon."

Flicking the card between his fingers he grinned.

"Absolutely, Detective." He stuffed it in his shirt pocket and headed out the same door Brandon exited.

Reaching his two-door, silver Mercedes, Jim took a seat in the driver's side. "I'm so sorry, Brandon."

He shook his head and stared out the windshield. "I have to call her sister. Her parents are going to be devastated."

Handing Martinez's card to him, Jim said, "He's expecting a call this afternoon. I think it's best if you cooperate and get ahead of this. I had Sam contact the legal department to try and find a good attorney if needed."

He quickly jolted his face towards him. "I don't need an attorney, Jim. I didn't do anything wrong."

"That wasn't what I was insinuating. But I highly suggest you take an attorney with you before speaking with Detective Martinez. You'd be a fool not to."

"I beg to differ. If I show up there to answer questions with an attorney, in their eyes, I'm as good as guilty!"

"If you don't you're setting yourself up. This is a *murder* investigation, Brandon."

"Well no shit. Pam was supposed to be at her sister's house and she turned up sleeping with the freaking fish." He rolled his eyes and took a deep breath before grabbing his hair with both hands and screaming out loud.

Jim sat patiently while his friend and colleague broke down. After taking a few deep breaths, Brandon straightened out his hair and attempted to put a game face on.

"What do you want to do, Brandon? I'll take you wherever you wanna go."

"Go back to the office. I need to talk to Sam."

Nodding his head, Jim buckled his seat belt and started the engine. They drove several blocks downtown back to the Tribune. Jim barely had the vehicle stopped before Brandon jumped out and sprinted into the building.

He ran up the stairs, down the hall, and into Samantha Brown's office, slamming the door behind him. The noise of the old wood and glass shook through to downstairs startling everyone in earshot. Sam jumped in her seat and immediately stood to receive the news from him. "Brandon, are you okay? Please say it wasn't Pam?"

He paced back and forth in front of her desk. "*Why?* Why on *earth* did you tell Detective Martinez I was with you?"

Her eyes looked up at him from under her full black bang, the remaining of her long hair flowing over her shoulders. "Oh my God. It was her, wasn't it?"

"Yes, Sam! It was Pam. For the love of God it was Pam and you told the man investigating her death that I was with you!"

She cupped her mouth with her right hand in shock. "Oh my God. Brandon, I'm so sorry!" She started around the desk to comfort him.

He raised his hands as a warning. "Please stop."

Her face became sullen. "I'm sorry, Brandon. It just came out! I thought I was helping you!"

"How the hell are you helping me by lying to a police detective? Please, do tell."

"Really Brandon? What the hell were you going to tell the man? 'Well, I worked late at the office and then I went home to cry again in my beer, *alone*.' I gave you an alibi. One that we both know you didn't have."

He stopped pacing and looked at her knowing she was right. "We're reporters, Sam. We seek the truth on a daily basis. We value the truth! I can't go talk to this detective and lie to his face!"

She grabbed him by the shoulders and forced him to look into her eyes. "You are the number one suspect here. The husband is always numero uno. If you don't have an alibi you know damn well they will build a case against you no matter what. For Christ sake, Brandon, you were just in court for domestic violence!"

He began pacing again mulling over the truth in her words.

"Look, I left before you did yesterday. I didn't speak or talk to anyone. You left here and went straight home, right?"

He nodded affirmatively.

"It's perfect! As long as we stick to the same story, everything will be fine. Everyone here knows you've been staying with me and everyone knows you guys are on the rocks. This isn't far fetched and I know you can sell it without a problem."

The look on his face showed he still needed to be convinced.

"Look at it this way; cops lie all the time to get what they need from someone. Well the shoe is on the other foot in this investigation. You just need to tell a little white lie to get them sniffing somewhere else and find the actual person who did this. It's that simple."

"I'll tell you what, Sam, if you think it's such an easy sell, you go talk to Detective Martinez for me and then you can bury my wife."

CHAPTER 8

$\mathcal{E}$lizabeth sat at her desk organizing her files for the upcoming week. There was a stack for letters that needed to be drafted and mailed in order to advise of pretrials and a stack for phone calls that needed to be made before the end of the day. Deciding to get the phone calls out of the way she picked up the receiver to dial a number. Getting a busy signal, she hung up the phone, closed the file and set it to the side for later.

As she opened her next file, her cell phone vibrated against the desk. She picked it up to see a text from Martinez. *Call me when you get a chance,* she read. She heard footsteps coming down the hall. *God, please let that be China!*

Peeking around the doorway, China said, "Hey! It's Friday!"

Looking up and smiling back, Elizabeth's eyes showed

signs of exhaustion. "If it's not the Friday of my retirement, I'm totally not interested."

"Awe, come on, Liz," said China as she plopped her files and her purse on the seat in the chair next to her.

Elizabeth's phone vibrated again from another text. *Liz, it's really important.* She took a deep breath and released it, making a motorboat noise between her lips.

"Who was that?"

"Martinez," she replied as if it hurt her to say his name.

"Okay, what's up?" She became defensive for a moment. "Did he do something wrong?"

"No, no. Nothing like that…"

"Okay, so, is it because you feel guilty about eating pork?" China laughed so hard her eyes welled with tears.

Elizabeth couldn't help but join in, shaking her head the entire time.

Her hand on her chest, China tried to calm herself. "Oh, oh-my-God. I'm sorry, Liz, it's just too easy!"

Trying not to laugh, Elizabeth couldn't keep a straight face. "This is serious!"

China took a tissue from Elizabeth's desktop and proceeded to pat the tears from under her eyes, careful not to smear her mascara. "Alright, alright. What's going on?"

Her phone vibrated again. "Shit. Hold on a second. I should really call him and see what's so important." She rolled her eyes placing the phone to her ear as China sat patiently checking her own phone.

His voice was melancholic. "Hey, I know you're busy

and probably trying to get some things out of the way before the weekend but I have some bad news."

"Well, I guess that's par for the course," she said shaking her head with a grim look on her face while she looked at China.

"I'm sorry, I just wanted you to hear it from me, I guess."

Her eyebrows scrunched together. "What's going on?"

"We found Pam DeFranco's body this morning, Liz."

"What?" she asked in disbelief.

"It's been confirmed. I'm so sorry, Liz. I know this was the last thing you wanted to hear. I'm afraid I'm going to be tied up this weekend with the investigation."

She placed her elbows on her desk to rub her forehead, her left hand still holding the phone to her ear.

"Liz?"

"I'm here." She sat back in her chair and let out a sigh of sadness mixed with disgust. "I wasn't expecting that at all. You do what you gotta do and I'll talk to you when I can?"

"Alright. Again, I'm sorry, Liz."

"You've been saying that too much lately."

"I'll talk to you soon," he said before hanging up.

China put her phone down. "So? What the hell was that all about?"

Before Elizabeth could answer they heard Marilyn scream from the front of the office. *"E-liz-a-beth!"*

China jumped. "Well crap on a stick. I don't think I'll ever get use to that damn cackle."

Elizabeth rolled her eyes. "I have received my summons."

Picking up her large purse and her files, she began to leave Elizabeth's office. Lifting up her free arm and waving it like a bird's wing she said, "Ca-caw!"

After letting out a giggle, Elizabeth sighed and stretched out her neck before meeting Marilyn in her office. Knocking her knuckle on the door a few times, she peeked her head in. Thankfully, Peggy wasn't around. She wanted to speak with Marilyn privately.

Looking up from the mess on her desk, Marilyn gave Elizabeth a slight smile. "Come on in, Elizabeth." Her face was fresh but looked tired from being in court all morning.

Grabbing the door to close it, she asked, "Do you mind?" Marilyn peeked over her wire-rim glasses and nodded her okay. She shut the door and took a seat in one of the leather chairs opposite her boss. Normally, being called into her office would call for a Valium, but Elizabeth kept telling herself she didn't do anything wrong. This time.

Marilyn set down her pen and removed her glasses from her face, placing them on the file she was currently working on. "Peggy told me about the blog post in the Tribune."

Taking a quiet deep breath she replied, "Well, I assumed that's what you wanted to talk to me about."

"*One* of the things I wanted to talk to you about.

Honestly, Elizabeth, I read the post and I can understand why Peggy was concerned."

It was typically unlike her to question authority, especially Marilyn's, but this time Elizabeth stood up for herself. "Marilyn, I really don't know why Peggy is up in arms about this. This isn't the first article the Tribune has written about this office. I explained to her my conversation with Pam DeFranco and she blew me off. Not only that, she sent me home for the day not even realizing the day *I* had, with every intention of leaving early anyway. I'm a little upset at her lack of empathy and how *she* handled the situation, frankly."

Marilyn sat quietly for a moment gathering her thoughts.

Before she could respond, Elizabeth continued. "What surprises me the most about this is that you, of all people, know how media can twist words to make something out of nothing to sell a few more papers or get a couple more subscriptions. I don't feel guilty or bad about what I told Pam. It was the truth. Her husband committed a crime and he had to answer for it. Hence, the whole 'bull by the horns' metaphor." She paused and looked into Marilyn's concerning eyes. "I can only be responsible for what I say. I am *not* responsible for how it's interpreted or misinterpreted for that matter."

Sitting back in her chair and crossing her legs she said, "I see where you are coming from. I do. But in our line of work, we really do need to be careful how we say things and to whom. Now, Peggy may not have handled it exactly how you would like but at this point in time she is your superior. She is in charge of your unit now, Elizabeth. I know you and China are not liking this change but it's one you're going to have to learn to live with."

Shifting uncomfortably in her seat, Elizabeth knew what she was saying was true. Well, part of it anyway. *Superior, pfft. Superior bitch, maybe.* "I'm not sure it matters now anyway. Martinez just called me and said they found Pam DeFranco's body this morning."

"Oh, dear. I'm sorry to hear that." She leaned forward and picked up her pen again, placing the end between her teeth as if it helped her think. "Any suspects yet?"

"I have no idea. He just said he would be tied up all weekend due to the investigation."

"Of course."

There was a strange silence between them before Marilyn chimed up again.

"I heard about what happened with the hearing, Elizabeth. I am so sorry."

"I guess I just wasn't meant to be there."

"I'm afraid that's the other issue I wanted to speak with you about."

Elizabeth stared curiously into Marilyn's aging eyes. "It was just a miscommunication. I didn't want to go. Martinez somehow talked me into it."

Her words were as slick as her dark hair pulled into the bun behind her head. "Martinez meant well and had you spoke at that hearing, it would have been good for you and probably... I'm sure it would have swayed the boards decision." Sitting forward in a caring manner, she folded her hands on top of her desk. "There's no easy way to say this, Elizabeth, but I wanted to tell you as soon as I got word."

The hair on her neck stood up and her pupils dilated in fear. Her heart began palpitating at the words she anticipated would leave Marilyn's lips next. Grabbing onto the arms of the chair she asked, "They're letting him out, aren't they?"

She nodded her head. "He's due to be released next Friday. I'm so sorry, Elizabeth. I wish I could have done more."

Her heart beat faster and stronger and she struggled between breaths. *This – this can't be happening.* Though it was difficult, she mustered a deep enough breath to ask, "I thought – they - had 30 days - to decide?"

"Up to 30 days. Are you okay? You're not looking so good, Elizabeth."

Her brain was on information overload. She felt a tingling sensation through her body as she tried to stand. Still trying to breath, her tan skin became a pale white before everything went dark.

When she came to, she felt a pillow under her head and saw Mildred's face. She was kneeling in front of her patting her face with cold, wet paper towels from the bathroom. Marilyn, China, and Constance stood hovering above them, speaking quietly.

Mildred smiled showing her white teeth behind red lipstick. "Hey, sweetie. Welcome back." She helped Elizabeth sit up and handed her a coffee cup filled with water and ordered her to take a sip. Constance whispered something to Marilyn and walked back to the main office area.

"Mildred? What happened?" she asked as she tried to stand.

"Whoa, hold on a sec." Helping her into the chair she explained, "You just had a teeny fainting spell." She handed the cup to Elizabeth. "Here, honey. Drink this and sit right there until you feel the dizziness wear off. If you need *anything* I'll be up front."

She took another sip of water. "Thanks, Mildred." Her conversation with Marilyn came rushing back to her. She stood up and held the back of the chair for balance.

Before leaving, China said, "Hey, I'll meet you in back, Liz."

Placing her hand on Elizabeth's shoulder Marilyn asked, "Are you okay?"

"I'm okay. I'm going to go back to my office and finish some things up."

"I'm sorry, Elizabeth. If there is anything I can do, please let me know. If you need to take the rest of the day -"

"I'll be okay, Marilyn. Thank you. I appreciate everything you've done." She was embarrassed. "I apologize for this," she said waving her hand. "It was just a little too much bad news for the day."

"No need to apologize, kiddo. I understand."

Elizabeth smiled shyly as she turned to walk back to her office. Walking through the front office, she was uncomfortable. She imagined everyone's thoughts about her situation and had a feeling they would be talking about her like they did the poor victims that passed through. The last thing she wanted was to be pitied.

China saw Elizabeth go into her office. She walked to the door, leaning her back against the frame. "Hey, sunshine. You okay?"

Holding onto the edge of the desk, she tilted her head back and took a deep breath. Tears formed in her eyes, one sliding from beneath her lash and down her cheek. Quickly wiping it away with her hand she said, "This has to be the worst day I've experienced in a while." She sat down in her chair and reached for her purse from under her desk fumbling through it for her pills.

China unfolded her arms and sat in the chair across from Elizabeth, offering her undivided attention.

Finding the pills she unscrewed the lid and popped one into her mouth, washing it down with a sip of water from her cup. Her face was full of anxiety. "He's getting out next Friday, China."

"I know he is, honey. I'm so sorry."

"What am I going to do? What if – I'm not sure – shit!" She rested her head on the back of the chair for a moment and shut her eyes giving the pill a chance to kick in and clear the clutter in her mind. Opening her eyes, she looked at China who was waiting patiently, allowing her to rant further. "Pam DeFranco is dead."

"Oh wow..." China's face dropped further. She was unsure of what else to say.

"Yeah." Shaking her head and rolling her eyes she said, "Martinez is going to be tied up all weekend and I'm sure Monday is going to be a shit show at court with all of this if an arrest is made. And now Steve." Her face was red and her eyes became watery again.

Attempting to change the negativity in the air, China burst with enthusiasm. "You know what we need? A girls night. Why don't you come over tonight? We can fire up the hot tub and drink some wine. No guns though. I don't want to shoot with you in your current state of mind." She was serious in a humorous way.

Elizabeth smiled and brushed another tear from her face. She really didn't want to be alone for the evening and she could never dismiss China's innate ability to lighten any mood. "You know, that sounds really awesome. But tomorrow is Saturday. We'll miss the beach. And you mean to tell me you don't have a date set up for a Friday night?"

"The beach will be there next week and I told you, Chester is old news." She rose from her seat. "Come over around 6-ish. I'll make dinner for us." She turned to her before going across the hall. "Everything's gonna be alright, Liz."

CHAPTER 9

Martinez sat at his desk recounting the earliest part of his investigation in his first report. He looked at his watch. It was after one o'clock and still no word from Brandon DeFranco. As he finished typing, Shawn walked in and sat at his desk across from the partition separating them.

"What's up man? Heard you had a crazy morning."

Looking up from his computer screen, Martinez nodded.

"Oh, come on. What, no dirty details for me?"

Still angry from their last encounter, Martinez lightly blew him off. "I'm just trying to get some stuff done, man."

Throwing his hands up Shawn said, "Okay, okay. It's cool. I get it." He turned away to face his computer.

Martinez shot a suspicious look Shawn's way. His wheels were spinning again. He pulled up his email and proceeded to write to Investigator McMurphy asking for more information regarding the email he never received, when his phone rang.

"Hey, Martinez. I have Brandon DeFranco down here, says you wanted to speak with him?"

"Thanks Alexander. I'll be right down." Hanging up the receiver, he saved the draft to his email and placed the password protection on his computer screen. He headed down the back stairwell that led to the police station lobby, where Brandon stood waiting for him.

Putting out his hand he said, "Mr. DeFranco, thank you so much for coming. Again, I am so sorry considering the circumstances."

Brandon refused his handshake. "Save the formalities, Detective. Can we just get on with it? I still have to arrange my wife's funeral."

"Of course. My apologies." Martinez led him into a five by eight foot interview room with two chairs and a table in between them. The walls were stark and cold. He shut the door behind them and the two men took a seat across from each other.

With his pad and pen in his hands, Martinez began going over his notes. "So, when we spoke this morning, Mr. DeFranco, you advised that you had not seen your wife since your court appearance yesterday morning, is that correct?"

Giving a head nod, Brandon kept a straight face. "That is correct."

"About what time did the two of you leave court?"

Rolling his eyes in thought, he answered, "Maybe around 11:30."

"When you left the courthouse, where did you go?"

"I went straight to work."

"Did your wife tell you where she was going?"

"She said she was going home."

"So, you didn't talk to her again for some time that day?"

"Nope."

"You said she sent you a text later in the evening?"

Leaning back in his chair, he sighed. "She text me around 8:30 saying she was going to her sister's house for a few days."

"And you were still at the Tribune at this time?"

"Yes, I had some hours to make up after being in court for a bogus charge."

He looked back at his notes for a moment. "And you say Samantha Brown was there with you, correct?"

"That is correct. Sam and I were working on a project together."

"Was any one else working late that night?"

"Not that I recall."

"And what time did you leave?'

"Actually, right around 8:30. We were packing up when Pam text me."

"Where did you go after that?"

"Sam and I went back to her place to grab some food and continue working."

"What did the two of you have to eat?"

Brandon rolled his head back to stretch out his neck and flung his hands on the table out of frustration. "Oh, come on, Detective! I did not kill my wife! I loved her. I would never do anything to hurt her."

"Well you do have two pending charges against you for doing just that, Mr. DeFranco."

The anger was building and he wasn't sure how much longer he could keep his composure. "Those are bullshit charges and you know it. My wife and I had a fight. Couples do fight. It got a little out of hand but I did not put my hands on my wife. I wouldn't, I *couldn't* do anything to hurt Pam."

"So tell me, Mr. DeFranco, who *would* want to hurt your wife?"

ELIZABETH PLACED the last dish in the dishwasher, closed it tight, and hit the on button. She turned around and leaned her back against the sink, gathered her blonde hair over one shoulder, and adjusted the bikini string around her neck. "I just don't get it. I read Marilyn's recommendation. What could he have possibly done in the past six years that justifies an early release? I mean, I get to deal with posttraumatic stress for the majority of my adult life, because of him, and he gets to skip out on 2 years? For what? Taking a few anger management classes over the years and proving he can be an 'upstanding citizen' in *prison*, of all places?"

China finished wiping down the island counter top and putting away the extra food, periodically looking at Elizabeth and nodding her head to show she was paying attention and understood her pain.

She waved her hands like a little Italian grandmother as she spoke. "We all know the prison system is a joke. There is no rehabilitation for these people. They send them away with these unrealistic expectations that they can mold them into contributing members of society by caging them like animals, forcing them to comply and conform, only to let them loose with felony records, completely unemployable, not to mention pissed off at the world, and their only recourse is to turn to the life that sent them there to begin with! Only this time, they get better at doing it." Taking a breath, she paused to fill her wine glass and take a sip.

Raising her glass to toast the absurdity, China said, "Welcome to the American criminal justice system." She grabbed the bottle and headed out to the patio.

Following behind, Elizabeth continued, "I just don't understand the bullshit psychology behind it all. It's no different than what we deal with everyday. Countless offenders and victims walking through the revolving door we call Silverton Municipal Court. The system doesn't have any answers or solutions. It does nothing but continue to place cheap Band-Aids on an infected, seeping wound."

China placed the bottle of wine on the shelf hanging on the side of the hot tub and slowly climbed into the jet-propelled water. She made herself comfortable and pulled her hair back, twisting it and clipping it up in a barrette. "I completely agree with you, Liz, but that cheap band aid is our job security, unfortunately."

Sighing at the harsh reality, she pursed her lips. "Tell that to Pam DeFranco's family."

Taking a sip of her wine and placing her glass on the shelf beside them, China spoke frankly. "Look, I know you're having a hard time with all of this, I mean, anyone would have a hard time with all the news you received today, but there's nothing you can do now about Pam. You just gotta ride this one out, Liz. Tell me I'm cold or harsh or what-have-you; this is one of the many hazards of our job. The one thing you *can* do something about is prepare yourself for Steve Robinson's release."

"What the hell is that supposed to mean? Prepare myself? Really, China?" She flung her arms over the side of the tub and shook her head from side to side before resting it on the plastic blow-up pillow, gazing at the stars above them. "You're right. I need to prepare." Maybe it was the warm, red wine clouding her perception. Maybe it was the water temperature of 100 plus degrees. Maybe it was a little of both that made her sit up and declare, "Can you give me one of your guns?"

A tad put off by her request, China replied, "Look, far be it from me to be the logical one, but don't you think you may want to start with renewing your protection order?"

Elizabeth rolled her eyes. "Because that has helped so

many people in the past. Come on, China. Where is this mystical voice of reason coming from?"

"I'm just saying, maybe you want to look at other options."

"I told you before, he doesn't have the address to the lake house. He's never been there. I get a protection order renewed, he knows right where to find me!"

"I still don't understand why you need to put your address on a protection order," China said with disdain.

"Well, China, because if you try and prosecute someone for being somewhere they aren't supposed to be, they actually have to know where exactly they aren't allowed to go." She sighed in disgust.

"Oh, I'm *sorry* Miss Attorney Lady. Forgive me for my ignorance." She rolled her eyes again and topped off her wine glass.

Elizabeth immediately felt bad for her ridicule. "I didn't mean it that way."

"Yes, you did. Whatever." Slumping into the tub a little further to massage her neck, China flung her bangs out of her eyes and quickly changed the subject. "Have you heard anything from Martinez?"

"Radio silence. Not that I blame him. I acted like such a spazz last night. So embarrassing," she said shaking her head and rolling her eyes.

"I almost forgot! You never did get to fill me in on all that. What happened?"

As her friend recounted her dream and the events that

followed, China's eyes grew wide with concern. "Damn, Liz!"

"Exactly! I mean, we ended up having a nice evening but it was still a little awkward, for me anyway. Ya know? I – I just don't know. It felt so good waking up to him but then after he left, my mind began to race and I pictured the worst."

"You know, I once heard that when women get hurt, it actually leaves a scar on their brain. Not on the heart, but on the *brain*."

Elizabeth's eyebrows inched closer together out of confusion. "What are you talking about?"

"No, wait! I'm not kidding! When we get hurt it leaves a ring on our brain, like trees that grow rings as they age."

"Where on earth did you read that?"

In a matter-of-fact tone she said, "I didn't read it, I heard it on the radio."

Elizabeth couldn't contain her laughter this time.

"Liz, I swear to you!"

"That is the most absurd thing I think I've heard in a while."

"No, think about it; look at how it affects us when we get hurt as opposed to most men. We're like devastated after a break up and they seem to move on with the speed and agility of a freaking super hero. On to the next conquest," she screamed as she laughed at her own words.

Looking to the star lit sky for a moment, Elizabeth gave it a thought. "I think there are some men out there who would disagree with you."

"Okay, maybe. Still, my point is you have scars on your brain, Liz. Your brain, your heart, whatever. Scars fade with time. But don't fool yourself into believing every man you encounter is going to treat you like Steve Robinson did. You can't let Martinez pay for something someone else did to you. That's not his burden to carry."

She looked into China's brown eyes, knowing she was right.

"Just call the man."

MARTINEZ WALKED into the bureau bright and early. He was clean-shaven and rested, looking more handsome than rugged. Shawn was sitting at his desk. Upon making eye contact, Martinez sat at his station without saying a word. Deciding to break the ice, Shawn spoke first. "So, what are you doing here on a Saturday morning? I thought the chief only worked me like a dog," he said with a sideways grin.

Looking up from over his computer screen, Martinez looked back down in silence.

Shawn was growing frustrated. He threw his hands up in the air before landing them on his thighs. "Look, man, I can't say I'm sorry enough. I don't know what happened, Martinez. Seriously. Chief's been all over my shit about this damn heroin epidemic and I was rushing around that morning..."

Pulling away from his computer, Martinez pushed his

chair back from his desk and sat with a cautioned look on his face, ready to hear out his colleague.

The lines in Shawn's face were remorseful. "I swear, I'm sorry."

Shaking his head, Martinez caved. "Look, this isn't all on you. You were right, I should have handled it myself."

"Naw, I told you I had your back. I should've come through." Pointing his finger at him he promised, "But I'm gonna make it up to you!"

Smiling, Martinez said, "Alright, you up for a little good cop bad cop?"

He laced his fingers, cupping his hands in his lap as his eyebrows shook devilishly. "That's what's up."

Excited, he stood from his seat and walked around to Shawn's space, leaning his buttocks against the desk. "Okay, so, Brandon DeFranco?"

Shawn nodded his head and rolled his eyes.

"Yeah, that one," he said shaking his head with a disgusted look on his face. "We pulled his wife's body from the lake yesterday morning."

His eyes were wide with intensity. "Wh*aaaat*? Get the hell outta here?"

"So far, he has a strong alibi. It seems pretty solid. Claims he was with a co-worker, a sexy co-worker at that, Samantha Brown. She's coming down this morning to 'confirm' his story that she was with him at *her* house."

"Okay, I'm with ya..."

"Well, the thing is, it's just not washing for me. He was just arrested a few nights ago and the wife got a TPO, kicked him out of his own house, right? So, the day before we find her, he claims she sent him a text at 8:30 PM saying she was going to her sister's house to stay for a few days. Knowing this, he leaves work at around the same time and goes to Samantha's house for the evening to work some more. That make any sense to you?"

Tilting his head back a bit, Shawn didn't need to think about it long. "Well, if my wife kicked me out of my house for a few days, then text me to let me know she was leaving for a while," pausing, his eyes squinted and he bit his bottom lip. "I think I just might be ready to chill on my own sofa and sleep in my own bed as soon as I could, work or not."

"Exactly. That is unless the sexy co-worker's bed is better. And if it is, we just may have a little motive."

"So, what time is this sexy little number supposed to be here?"

"She should be downstairs any minute now."

Excited, Shawn jumped out of his chair. "Let's do this! I get bad cop right?"

Martinez shook his head and headed out the door, Shawn following behind him. As they reached the end of the stairwell and opened the heavy door into the police lobby, Samantha was coming in from the main entrance. She was wearing a tight, black V-neck shirt showing just enough cleavage and a pair of khaki Capri's.

Whispering to Martinez, Shawn said, "Da-yum!"

Reaching out his right hand, Martinez greeted her. "Miss Brown, thank you so much for coming down. This is Detective Johnson. He'll be joining us today, if that's okay with you?"

She smiled, her semi-crooked teeth peering through her dark mauve lipstick. "It's no problem. Anything to help Brandon out. Please, just call me Sam."

After being shown to the interview room, Martinez took a seat across from Sam setting his notebook on the table. Shawn remained standing off to the side in order to gauge her facial expressions and step in when he felt the need.

Martinez placed the recorder on the table and pressed play. "Obviously, this conversation will be recorded as per our policy."

She nodded her head, placed her iPhone on the table next to his recorder and began to record as well. She winked at him. "I have my own policy."

Shaking his head in response he turned to Shawn, "You good with that?"

Before Shawn could answer, Sam stated matter-of-factly, "It's my Constitutional right, detectives." Her blue eyes glared at them through her black eyeliner.

"Okay then." Martinez looked at his notes for a moment. "So, I guess we can start with this past Thursday. You were working this day?"

"I work everyday, Detective," she said with a slight smile of defiance.

Shawn was irked by her current demeanor and couldn't wait to step in but he let Martinez continue. "Let me reword that; you were working at the Tribune on

Thursday? And if so, did you happen to see when Brandon arrived that day?"

"I *was* at the office and I think Brandon got there sometime before lunch."

"Would you be able to tell me if he was at the tribune for the entire day?"

"Actually, yeah. We've been working on an assignment together and it took up the majority of the day Thursday. We had some catching up to do since he had to be in court the entire morning." Her lips curled with annoyance.

Not changing his pleasant, good-cop tone he asked, "Do you know what time he left for the day?"

Looking him square in the eyes she said, "I do."

Not being able to take her attitude anymore, Shawn spoke up. "Enough with the brazen bullshit already and just answer the questions."

"I *did* answer the question, Detective."

Moving forward he placed his hands down hard on the table startling her. "What time did Mr. DeFranco leave the Tribune Tuesday and can you vouch for his whereabouts after the fact?"

Her temper began to flare a bit but she didn't look away from his gaze. "I'm not sure I need to put up with this type of questioning."

Still centered and calm, the interview was going just as he planned. "Sam, you'll have to forgive my partner here, he didn't get his coffee this morning." Shawn backed off and retreated to his space against the wall. "Can you please tell us what time Brandon left for the day and if you know where he went afterward?"

Her eyes remained on Shawn as she moved her head slowly towards Martinez. "Brandon and I left the office around 8:30 and we went back to my place to order in some food and finish some things with regards to our assignment."

"And what time did he leave your place that evening?"

"He didn't." Glancing at Shawn she continued, "He fell asleep on the couch and we left for work together the next morning."

"Sam, can you tell me how long you have known Brandon DeFranco?"

Rolling her eyes to think for a moment, she said, "I don't know, about three years I guess."

"The two of you close?"

Shrugging her shoulders she replied, "Pretty close. I'm basically his work wife."

Although his facial expression didn't change, a red flag went off for Martinez and he knew Shawn would be chiming in again soon.

"Did you know his wife well? The two of you get along?"

She sighed. "Pam and I didn't talk much. She did her own thing and I don't think she liked Brandon working so much. They were having problems, you know. Hence, he was staying at my place."

Martinez continued taking notes. He looked up at her

from his pad, tapped his pen, and casually asked, "So, he had been staying with you for how long?"

"Since last Saturday when she called the police and kicked him out of his house," she said bitterly.

"Sounds like you might have a jealous beef with the little wifey," said Shawn antagonizing her.

Squinting her eyes at him defensively, Sam growled back, "Pam was a snotty bitch and hated the fact that he and I had the relationship we did. *She* was the jealous one." She quickly realized she allowed him to get the best of her. She had said too much.

Taking a breath she looked at Martinez. His face was sympathetic but his eyebrows curled with curiosity. "Look, I'm sorry for what happened to her but she was no angel in all of this." She grabbed her phone and stopped the recording, shoving it into her bag. She stood up and wrapped her purse around her shoulder. "I have work to do. Have a good day, Detective." Shooting Shawn a nasty look she walked out the door.

The two men sat in silence until she had exited the police station. Shawn walked around the table and took a seat across from Martinez. He placed his hands behind his head and sprawled his legs out like the alpha male who had just claimed his territory. "Well she's a pistol, aye!"

Sitting back in his chair Martinez smirked. "You ain't kidding. I told you this whole alibi of DeFranco's isn't making any sense. Why would he continue to stay at a 'friend's' house when the wife left? And 'work wife'? What the hell is that? Either she's screwing him, or she desperately wants to."

Shawn's face lit up. "Ah man, can you imagine? I bet she's a bear in bed!"

Lifting his masculine chin he asked, "Seriously, Johnson, what do you make of it?"

Scratching the stubbly grays on the side of his head, he said, "I'm with you, man. It doesn't make sense. Something's rotten in Denmark."

Feeling guilty for previously being so angry with him, Martinez was grateful. "That was nice work, Johnson. I appreciate your help."

"Awe, don't go getting all sentimental on me now. It was fun. We should do this more often." He glanced at his watch. "You hungry? Wanna grab a burger at Jimmy's?"

He thought about it for a minute. "You know, that's sounds awesome about now. Just let me make a phone call."

Rising from his position, Shawn scooted the chair under the table. "I'll meet ya there with a cold beer waiting for you."

Once Shawn left the room, Martinez hit Elizabeth's contact number in his phone. It went straight to voicemail. "Uh, hey, Liz, sorry I've been so tied up. Um, nothing new here, well kind of. Weird, weird, people. Investigation is moving along though. Me and Johnson are about to grab some grub. I just thought I'd try you real quick. I hope we can get together soon. Uh, okay. I'll talk to you later. Bye."

CHAPTER 10

$\mathcal{A}$rriving at her desk just before eight o'clock, Elizabeth was ready to get her Monday started. She assumed no arrest had been made in the DeFranco case since there were no further updates from Martinez. She still felt guilty about not returning his call. Immediately brushing off her thoughts, she pushed her hair back behind her ears, logged into her computer, and began preparing for court when her phone rang.

"Victim Assistance, this is Elizabeth."

"Good morning! It's Andrea."

"Hey Andrea, what's up?"

"I have a lady up here, Janet Burrows, would like to speak with you. Says she's Pamela DeFranco's sister."

Her heart sinking into her chest she whispered, "Shit."

Andrea still heard her. "What should I tell her?"

After pausing for a moment, Elizabeth sighed. "Just give me a minute. I'll be right there." Hanging up the receiver, she rubbed her forehead wondering how this conversation was going to go. Speaking quietly to herself, she said, "It's way too early for this." Pulling herself out of her chair, she managed to muster up the energy to walk to the front of the office. Taking a deep breath, she opened the heavy door leading into the lobby.

A tall, thin woman with long brown hair streaked with highlights turned to greet her. "Elizabeth Strong?"

She doesn't look anything like Pam, was her initial thought. Pam reminded her of a schoolteacher. This lady was more attractive and professional in a classy way. "Hello, Miss Burrows, is it?" She was hesitant. Typically, she was the one contacting family members, not the other way around.

Closing her eyes for a moment, she shook her head to stop her eyes from welling up. "I was away on business when my parents called me to inform me my sister, Pam DeFranco, had been killed." Breathing deeply, she flung her hair off her shoulder. "I'm sorry. I'm not quite sure what I'm supposed to do here or what happens now, but..." She reached into the front pocket of her Coach bag and pulled out a business card, handing it to Elizabeth. "I found your card while going through her things this weekend. I'm afraid I felt more comfortable coming here than going to the police station."

Elizabeth looked down at her card and back up to Janet, nodding sympathetically. "Of course. Let's go back to my office where we can talk." She waved at Andrea on the other side of the bulletproof glass window as a sign to buzz them in. She led Janet down the hall and into her office, shutting the door behind them for privacy.

"Please have a seat," said Elizabeth as she sat down in her chair. She wasn't sure at this point who should start the conversation but it seemed only natural to begin. "I'm so sorry for your loss."

Trying to remain strong, a tear fell from Janet's eyelash. Elizabeth reached over and placed a box of tissue in front of her. "Thank you," Janet said with a sniffle before continuing. "Pam had contacted me last week after she and Brandon had their little blow out. I knew they had been having problems and I told her she could stay at my place while I was gone. I left Sunday afternoon for Boston and she could have had the place to herself to sort some things out. Then she sent me a text and told me everything was okay; they were working things out. I never expected *this*. Can you help me fill in any of the blanks over the past week?"

Normally, Elizabeth would refrain from discussing her interactions with a victim due to issues of confidentiality. Normally also meant that the victim she interacted with was still alive. "Well, I met with Pam last Saturday after she called the police. After speaking with her, she decided it was best to obtain a temporary protection order to keep Brandon out of the house for the time being.

"She seemed scared, frustrated, and confused. After I explained everything to her, she decided she needed some space. Of course, it didn't last long because on their court date, she was sitting next to him in his defense ready to drop the charges and basically told me to leave her alone. The very next day, they found her body. I'm afraid that is all the information I have. I was hoping maybe you could be of more help to *us*. Did you speak with Pam on a regular basis?"

Wiping her nose with the tissue and crumbling it up in her fist, she tossed her hair out of her face and took a breath. "Pam and I were always pretty close. She and Brandon have always had a strange relationship. I always wondered what she saw in him. He was a journalist trying to make a career for himself and she wanted nothing more than to be a mother.

"They had toyed with the idea for a while, but he wouldn't budge. Over the past few years we grew more distant. I mean we both have lives we're trying to live. I talked to her a while back and she was tired of waiting for him to really settle down and start a family. She told me she had met someone else." She rolled her eyes. "I tried to talk some sense into her but she was on another plain. Last week, the last time I talked with her, she and Brandon had reached their boiling point, she told him about her affair. That's what set him off. And rightfully so! I told her she was playing with fire but she wouldn't listen to me. And now she's dead," she said bluntly as she patted under her eyes with the tissue.

The only word Elizabeth heard was 'affair'. "So, Pam was having an affair? Do you know how long it had been going on for?"

Breathing in deeply and then releasing she said, "Gosh

I don't know. Six months or so? The icing on the cake was she had just found out she was pregnant. When she called me, she informed me I was going to be an aunt." Janet stopped herself from choking up. "I was excited for her. She told me everything was going to work out and she was going to finally live the life she really wanted. Funny thing is, I don't think she even knew who the father was. At least she didn't divulge that information to me."

Trying to hide the surprised look on her face, she pried further. "Janet, do you think Brandon could have done this? I hate to say it, but to me it sounds like he had a pretty decent motive."

"Honestly, I don't know what to think anymore. I never thought my brother-in-law would put his work before my sister let alone do anything like this. I never thought my sister would cheat on her husband. I certainly never thought I would get a phone call telling me my sister turned up dead in Lake Erie. I haven't had a real heart to heart with Pam in years. All I know is she was in a weird place for a while and all I could do was be there for her whenever she called me."

Shaking her head, Elizabeth said, "I cannot tell you how sorry I am, Janet." She paused a moment. "You understand I am going to share all this with the investigating officer?"

Janet swallowed the reality hard, her throat making a noise before she answered. "I understand. Like I said, I wanted to speak with you rather than the police on this matter. I appreciate you taking the time to talk with me."

"Of course. I will be here throughout this entire process, Janet. However, I'm afraid once I share this with Detective Martinez, he *will* want to speak with you personally."

She closed her eyes for a moment and nodded. "I'm aware of that as well. Do they have any idea what happened? I have only talked with my parents since returning home. I mean I saw Brandon long enough for him to let me in the house and to offer my assistance. He was extremely quiet. I can only imagine what he is going through right now. I tried to be receptive to him but he was so – distant." She shook her head as if trying to shake off a bad feeling. "I don't want to make any assumptions, but I don't know. It's such a crazy, tragic situation and I'm entirely too close to it to make any judgments."

Surprised by her logical reasoning and willingness to give her brother-in-law the benefit of the doubt, Elizabeth advised, "I'm afraid I haven't heard anything yet. They are still investigating at this point. The one thing I can tell you is I will keep you as informed as I can. Can I ask you one more thing, Janet?"

"Of course, anything."

Elizabeth readied her pen on her notebook and asked, "Do you have any idea who Pam was having an affair with?"

WALKING INTO THE BUREAU, Shawn grabbed a stack of papers from the fax machine, flipped through them, and lightly tossed them on Martinez's desk. "All yours, my man. Looks like you're gonna have a busy day." He winked.

He smirked. "Yeah, no kidding. Thanks, Johnson."

Sitting down in his chair as if it was a recliner in his living room, he asked, "Any break in your homicide yet?"

Shaking his head and taking a break from his paperwork, he sighed. "Nope. I talked with her parents and coworkers on Friday. Everyone had the same thing to say about her; nice girl with no enemies and didn't really have much of a life. The husband is the only suspect right now."

Shawn quickly corrected him. "Unless he's banging that sexy reporter. Then wouldn't you consider her a suspect as well?"

"Good point. But good luck getting either one of them to give up that information, if it's true." Flashing the papers Shawn gave him, he said, "I'm hoping the phone records will give me a little something. Otherwise, I got nothing. How 'bout you? What do you have going on this week?"

He rolled his eyes. "Same old smack heads, different day."

They both turned their chairs in the direction of the door upon hearing Chief Holden clear his throat as he entered the room. He held a large cup of coffee in one hand, his other stuffed in his left front pants pocket. "Good morning. Hope you all had a nice weekend.

Although I know you spent half of it here." Shawn gave Martinez another roll of his eyes. "You're work *is* appreciated, Johnson."

"Well thanks for letting us know, Chief."

He raised his mug and took a sip of his coffee. "So, word on the wire is one of our favorite felons is due to be released by the end of the week."

Shawn scrunched his forehead in frustration showing his wrinkles and asked, "Oh yeah, who's that?"

Martinez chimed in, "This should be interesting."

"I'm afraid just a little more interesting for you, Martinez," he said looking at him over the top of his black frames. "Steve Robinson was granted parole. He's due to be released Friday."

The look on his face was pure shock. "Friday? They just had the damn hearing!"

Shawn hung his head slightly as if waiting for the room to explode.

Shaking his head and holding his hands out waiting for an explanation, Martinez said, "Chief? Has Elizabeth heard about this?"

He breathed deeply and hung his head as well for a moment. He scratched the top of his head and pushed his long fingers through his white locks. Looking up at Martinez he informed him, "I can only tell you what I know and at this point it ain't much. I've seen parole approvals go quickly but this has to be a record. As far as Elizabeth, I assume Marilyn informed her. I guess I figured you would have talked to her this weekend."

Guilt washed over him. "I – I've been so busy with this investigation, I haven't even touched base with her. I mean I did but... Shit!"

"Well, I'll let the two of you sort that out. In the meantime, Johnson, I need you to get a hold of Robinson's parole officer. We're gonna want to get a head of the game. Far as I know Robinson gave a Silverton address. He'll do an about-face and when he does, I want to be ready. We need to be updated by his PO with every meeting he has and I want you or someone from this department at every random search of his residence. Also, find out how often we *can* conduct a random search and make sure it's done. Keep a close eye on him."

Giving the chief a nod, Shawn rolled his chair into his desk and went back to work. Martinez immediately spoke up. "I want in on this, Chief."

He took a big gulp of his coffee, savoring the flavor for a moment. He pushed his lips together and stared into his cup thinking. "Now I'm not sure that's such a good idea, Martinez."

"Oh, come on! Chief, I need this."

"You're too close to this. The last thing I need is Robinson reverting back to his old ways and a charge not sticking because you have a conflict of interest or heaven forbid he dream up some harassment lawsuit against the department. I don't need the headache. Johnson's got this handled. He's drug enforcement. You're homicide. Period."

"Seriously? I wouldn't jeopardize my career or the department for that asshole. I just -"

He turned his back to Martinez and headed towards his office. "End of discussion. Johnson will keep you abreast of the situation. Right, Johnson?" With that he walked out.

Shawn turned to Martinez. "Don't worry man. I got this! I'll keep you updated. Besides, we roll together all the time." He shrugged his shoulders. "Once in a while I may have to make a stop and you just happen to be there." He gave Martinez a wink and looked back at his computer screen.

Martinez pursed his lips thuggishly and slowly nodded his head. Returning to his own computer, he opened his email from Investigator McMurphy, which read, "Detective Martinez, please find below the original message I sent you regarding the date and time change of the parole hearing for Steve Robinson. If you have any other questions, please do not hesitate to contact me." He was frustrated to see the message was indeed sent to his email address the previous Monday. Somehow, it was never received. The clock on his computer read 8:45 am. He knew Elizabeth would be downstairs getting ready for the influx of victims at municipal court. "Hey, Johnson, I'm gonna head downstairs and make a phone call then see if I can't catch up with Liz real quick, in case Chief comes looking for me."

Almost irritated by the interruption, Shawn didn't look up from his work. "Yeah, sure, man."

Martinez rose from his chair, grabbed his cell phone and headed for the stairwell. His feet slid down the stairs with agility. Reaching the heavy, steel door, he pulled the handle and walked through the police station lobby and past the records window to outside. He pulled up a contact on his phone and hit send.

"Yo, Medicine Man, here. What's your ailment?"

"Miles, it's Martinez. I need a favor."

"Sup, Martinez." Miles Murphy was parked on the side of the road and looked up over his dark sunglasses at the flashing police lights in the rearview mirror of his Cadillac. "You be like my guardian Angel, brotha. Da big man upstairs be lookin' out, my man. Yo, whachu need?"

"I got a job for you, Miles. It's pretty big and it may take a while."

The beat cop approached Miles' vehicle and came up to the window, rapping on it with his knuckle.

"Da-yum! My Angel always know when to show *up*. Ima need somethin' from you first. You gon' have to call off the dogs, my man. Yo, hold up, hold up." He pushed the button on the driver's side, the window slowly disappearing into door. He pulled his shades down his nose and looked directly into the cop's eyes. "Yo, occifer, Ima need your badge numba, brotha, 'cause I just got my get-out-of-jail-free card."

Martinez became frustrated on the other end of the phone. "Damn it, Miles!"

"Yo, take down this numba. I got some bidness to take care of after I roll up outta here. Meet you at our regular for lunch, a'ight?"

After writing down the officer's badge number,

Martinez returned to the lobby and entered the code into the door lock leading to the station. He went straight to dispatch and ordered Lacy to call off Officer Smith who had Miles pulled over. Once that was handled, he walked across the hall to municipal court. Walking into the court lobby, he saw China finishing up with someone. As soon as she was done he went over to her. "Hey, China, how's it going?"

Giving him a flirtatious look and flexing her eyebrows at him she said, "*Hey*, Martinez!"

"Is Liz around?"

"Yeah, she's here. She's probably in Traffic making copies.

"Thanks!" He spun around and walked past the probation department to the Traffic office where most DUI offenders went to receive their instructions. Peeking in the door he saw Elizabeth at the copy machine. He leaned against the frame and watched her wishing they weren't at work.

Upon feeling his presence, Elizabeth turned to the door and caught his eyes. Her stomach fluttered and her body tingled at the sight of him. She smiled wide. "Hey, you."

He leaned his head against the doorframe. "Hey yourself. You gotta second?"

She continued to look at him while pushing buttons on the machine as if she was preprogrammed. "Of course. I was going to look for you when I was done here. Just let me finish this up, okay?"

Giving her a head nod, he continued to admire her.

The copier continued to push out paper until Elizabeth realized it seemed to be producing more than she may have needed. She looked at the screen that read '100' copies. She frantically began pushing buttons trying to make it stop. "Shit. Shit!"

In full on defense mode he ran to her rescue. "What happened?"

Giggling, she said, "I think I hit 100 instead of ten! Oh shit, it won't stop! Ha ha!"

They both continued to hit the buttons on the copy machine until it stopped spitting out paper. "Holy crap, thanks! I really don't think my victim has 100 places she visits regularly. Ten copies should do it!" Catching each other's eyes, she said, "Let me drop these off and I'll be right back okay?"

Elizabeth met a young girl in the lobby and explained to her to keep a copy in her purse, in the glove box of her vehicle, and to give a copy to work and any other place she frequented on a regular basis. She explained, "If you need to call the police due to him violating the protection order, you want to make sure there is always a copy available. Be prepared and make them do their job. Don't give them any excuses to overlook it. This is a court order and he has to obey it. So do the police. Okay? I'll talk to you soon." The girl thanked her and went on her way.

Martinez hung out in the background watching every move she made and hung onto every word she spoke.

When she walked up to him, he said, "You know, you're really good at what you do."

She rolled her eyes. "Maybe. I just wish it made as much of a difference as I think it did."

"I think you'd be surprised. You know, you do a lot for those women."

Being modest, she said, "I sure hope so. So, what's up?"

They began slowly walking away from the courtroom to a quiet part of the building. Hanging his head shamefully, he said, "Sorry I was tied up all weekend."

She shook her head. "It's okay. I hung out with China most of the weekend. It's been a while since we've had some girl time, and I really needed it, so no worries."

Rubbing the scruff on his chin, he wasn't quite sure how to bring up the subject. He stopped her in the middle of the hall. "Liz, I should have been there for you this weekend and I wasn't. I'm sorry."

Breathing in deeply, she knew she wouldn't be able to hide it from him for long. She backed up against the wall and held her files close to her. "I take it you heard?"

He placed his hand against the wall above her head, his body hovering over her protectively. "Of course I heard. One of the biggest dealers in town is getting paroled, Liz. Not only that, Chief Holden gave me his file months ago when Johnny Warren started harassing you. Of course I'm going to get word of his release. The question is how are we going to handle this?"

Letting out a deep breath she explained, "He's getting out. What's there to handle?" There was a concerned crease in his forehead that made her melt. Shaking her head she looked into his deep brown eyes. "I can't do it, Angel."

He titled his head in a begging manner. "All day long you talk these women into protecting themselves, yet, you can't do that for yourself? I don't get it."

Relaxing her grip on the files in her chest, she became surefooted. "What you and China seem to forget is that the women who walk through those doors need protection from men who currently live in their homes. The men and women China deal with don't live with each other, but they *do* know *where* they live. Steve doesn't know where I live and I'd like to keep it that way as long as I can."

"Exactly. How long do you think that's gonna last. If Robinson wants to find you, and you can bank on that fact, he's going to find you, Liz. If you renew the protection order, I can hand deliver it to him before he even leaves the gates. Trust me, it would be my pleasure." He gave her an evil smirk.

"I know you and China both mean well, but I certainly don't want to make things any easier for him." Leaving the security of the wall behind her, she gave him one last look, ordering him to let it go. "I think I'll pass. Can we talk in the interview room?" Walking into the room she tossed her files onto the table and grabbed the handle to the door, nodding her head slightly for him to follow. "I had an interesting conversation this morning with Pam DeFranco's sister."

The serious expression on his face remained unchanged. With pep in his step he entered the room, Elizabeth shutting the door behind them. They sat down across from each other and she began filling him in. Martinez listened intently as he took notes. She sat back frustrated. "You know, I never made Pam out to be a cheater. I wish I could gauge people a little better."

Twirling his pen in his hand he said, "So, Brandon finds out his wife has a little side piece and freaks out. That explains why we were called out there Saturday. Did he know about the alleged pregnancy?"

Shrugging her shoulders she assumed, "From what Janet said, it sounded like she just found out. Maybe she confronted him with the pregnancy and wanted to leave. Things were already heated. Can you imagine if he found out his wife was pregnant not even a week after hearing about an affair? Sounds like motive to me." She sat back in the chair and crossed her legs.

Tapping his pen against the table his mind wandered. "That sounds totally plausible. However, what if she and Brandon decide to work things out and he demands she break things off with her little fling?" He gave Elizabeth a sly grin. "That's the thing about affairs. The marriage usually wins in the end. And sorry for me, I have another suspect and theory to investigate. So who's this boyfriend anyway?"

Smacking her lips, she said, "Unfortunately, Janet didn't seem to know that little piece of information. When siblings tend to disagree with your decisions and/or lifestyle, you in turn tend to share as little information as possible while still letting them know you're okay." She batted her lashes. "I speak from experience."

"Fair enough." He thought for a moment before becoming excited. "You wanna go to a funeral?"

Offset by his odd request, she asked, "Are you asking me on a date? To a funeral? How macabre." She snorted through her nose.

Tilting his head to the side he said, "Well, when you put it that way." He smirked. "I just need another set of eyes and Johnson's got something else going on." Without mentioning Robinson, he looked at his watch and continued, "I figure the DeFranco and Burrows families should be burying their loved one soon and my guess is the boyfriend is going to show up not long after they all say their goodbyes. He's certainly not going to show up to mourn with the husband. Be a good time to find out who this mystery lover is."

She squinted her eyes showing contemplation of his logic. Biting the inside of her cheek she hesitated before nodding in agreement.

He smacked his hand on the table in excitement. "Alright then! I gotta go meet my CI about another matter. How 'bout you finish up here and I'll swing by and pick you up in say, an hour?"

Gathering her files from the table she said, "Bring sandwiches. I don't need it getting back to Peggy how I failed to follow her orders and stick within my job description. I'm already on thin ice."

Giving her a look of understanding, he replied, "Hey, I'm just taking my girl out to lunch." He stood up, leaned over the table, and kissed her on the forehead before walking out.

Shaking her head, she sighed and slightly smiled. *He is sooo going to get me in trouble...*

~

PULLING in across the street from the Silverton Fish Company, Martinez parked his sedan in one of the open spaces on Shoreline Drive and exited his vehicle. After looking both ways, he crossed the street, his eyes scanning the establishment. Miles was seated by himself at a picnic table facing the bay. He was dressed in Detroit Red Wings attire with blue jeans and red Jordan's to match his jersey.

Martinez inconspicuously walked up to the side of the table looking out to the bay and said, "You stick out like a sore thumb, Miles."

Dunking a piece of his fish into a container of tartar sauce he laughed. "Ha Haaa!" He stuffed a bite into his mouth and licked the grease from his fingers. "Mm, mm, mm! Best perch this side of Lake Erie." Taking a sip of soda from the straw in his to-go cup he said, "Ya'll can't keep every thang for the yuppie white folk. Downtown becomin' some gentrified bullshit. Fo' real 'doh. SPD done kicked out Mr. Henry from his spot down the street. What's wrong? White folk don't like BBQ?"

"Mr. Henry didn't have the proper permits or inspections from the health department, Miles."

"Yeah, well, Mr. Henry now South side by 'da casino dealing wit drunks and poor folk looking for a handout. Got robbed the other day, too. He been servin' BBQ in this town long before that jacked up sushi place shoved itself down our throats. But the white gyro man still got his spot and he doin' *good*!" He looked at Martinez from under his dark sunglasses.

Cocking his head to the side, he caught Miles' eyes. "What do you want Miles?"

Pulling his sunglasses down his nose a bit, he said, "You know what I want, Martinez; for Silverton, Ohio to once again be an equal opportunity for small bidness owners. What*chu* want, my man?"

Taking a deep breath, he looked back out at the bay. "Steve Robinson is getting released from prison this week."

Stopping himself from finishing his last bite of perch, he placed it back into the Styrofoam container, wiping his hands with a napkin. "So, it's true?"

"Yep. What I need to know is, who helped him. He just had his parole hearing last week. There is no way he would have been approved and scheduled for release this fast without some kind of help. There's a dirty cop somewhere and I need details. I need a name."

Cleaning up his mess on the table, Miles laughed out loud. "A dirty cop? Naw, man. You trippin'! Dem's hard to come by. Ha ha! Dirty cop," he repeated while shaking his head. As he headed to the large trash bin, Martinez walked in front of him.

"This isn't a joke Miles. I know Robinson's release affects you too *wit' your bidness* and all." He grabbed the container from Miles and tossed it in the trash. "Get me the dirt on Robinson's release. I'll get Mr. Henry doing business again downtown."

Miles looked Martinez in the eyes knowing he could count on his word. "A'ight. Bet."

CHAPTER 11

Martinez slowly pulled into the cemetery drive off Bogart Rd. and kept his speed below the posted 10 mph. Elizabeth sat quietly as the sacred monuments rolled past them, the sun gleaming off the granite and marble. An old man sitting on a cement bench caught her eye. He appeared to be reading a book aloud. Possibly to his long lost wife, buried under the earth just feet in front of him. She thought of her parents. *At least they're together.*

Feeling the sadness in the air, Martinez turned to see Elizabeth gazing out the window and asked, "Hey, you okay?"

Shaking off the heavy feeling she snapped out of it. "Sure. Just not much for graveyards, ya know?"

He was angry with himself for being so insensitive. "Damn, Liz. I'm sorry. Do you wanna go back?"

She shook her head negatively. "It's not your fault.

Honestly, I didn't think I would be bothered so much. It's just a little hard seeing so many symbols of peaceful sorrow. It's so contradicting. You can't possibly be sad and know peace at the same time."

Never giving it much thought before, he understood her point. "I suppose not." Just up over the small hill he noticed a line of vehicles with funeral flags clinging onto their front ends and a large group of people hovering over a grave as a metal device lowered Pam DeFranco's casket into the ground. He pulled off to the side of the road and put the car in park. "Maybe a peaceful sorrow isn't such an oxymoron. I mean the dead are at peace. It's only the living who are sad. The two actually can co-exist, however unfair that may be."

She propped her elbow on the inside of the doorframe and rested her head in her hand. "Hmm. You may be onto something there, Angel. But it seems very unfair."

Reaching around to the back seat, he grabbed the plastic bag from Silverton Fish Company with two Styrofoam meal boxes and set it between them on the console. Elizabeth looked at him strangely. "I thought I smelled perch."

He winked. "I told you I was just taking my girl to lunch."

Taking another look at their surroundings, she said, "I hate to say, I'm really not that hungry at the moment. Sorry."

He shrugged his shoulders. "No worries." He pulled a sandwich out and grabbed a napkin. "But please don't consider me an insensitive jack ass." He took a large bite out of the sandwich, which left a smidge of tartar sauce in the corner of his mouth before he wiped it away. With a mouth full of perch he said, "Looks like the family is starting to filter out."

Elizabeth watched as all the people walked away from the gravesite back to their vehicles. Brandon DeFranco was arm in arm with an older woman. She figured her to be Brandon's mom or possibly the mother of the deceased. "Those poor people. It's just so tragic. Do you think he did it?"

Gulping down some of his soda, he shrugged his shoulders. "I don't know. Too soon to tell at this point. Of course, if Pam was sleeping around and got knocked up by another guy, couldn't be a better motive. Well, I take that back. Samantha Brown could be another nail in the coffin. No pun intended."

Her forehead crinkled together. "Samantha Brown?"

Raising his chin towards the people he said, "See that foxy little chic in the black dress with the long black hair walking behind Brandon?"

She smirked and flexed her eyebrows at him. "Foxy huh?"

"Well she is!"

Elizabeth squinted as if it helped her see better from a hundred feet away. "I guess I'll take your word for it."

"I'm guessing she and Brandon have a thing. She called herself his work wife."

"Well that doesn't make any sense. If they were both

cheating on each other why kill Pam? Why not just get a divorce and they both be on their merry way?"

Pointing a French fry into the air like a conductor wand he said, "Exactly, my dear Watson!"

She flirted with him with her smile, loving the fact he found such comfort in a character born to him out of such a terrible childhood. One that obviously played some type of role in who he became.

Chewing his last bite, he stuffed the remnants of his food and container back into the bag and crunched it up, throwing it into the back seat. "You know, even though I was busy with the investigation this weekend, why did it seem like you were avoiding me?"

Her eyes flickered anxiously. She took a breath and leaned on the headrest. "It's not that I was trying to. There was just too much running through my head. With Pam, then – then Steve. I was just beat."

"See, right there. You paused. You were about to say something. Did I do something wrong?"

She turned her head towards him, her eyes sad with adoration. "You only became my worst nightmare."

Taken aback he said, "Wow. That's a first." He bit his bottom lip, slowly releasing it as he lowered his head.

Open mouth insert foot, Liz. "The other night when you came over, I was all out of sorts. Before you got there, I was in the bath and had an 'episode', or so my shrink likes to call them." She shook her head embarrassed at herself. "I dreamt that you turned into Steve. You turned into him but you were still you. I mean, I saw *you*, but all I heard and all that happened were only things *he* would say and do." She grabbed her temples and rubbed them hard. "I know I don't make any sense. I'm sorry."

Resting his elbow on the armrest, he rubbed his chin for a moment before turning to look at her. "You know that would never happen, right?"

Looking out towards Pam's grave she said, "Well, that's what my conscious likes to tell myself. My subconscious, however, makes up it's own stories." She met his eyes and asked, "I'm a train wreck waiting to happen, Martinez. Are you sure you wanna get any more involved? She shook her head and looked back out at the gravesite. "I really couldn't blame you if you want to back out."

"Tell you what, how 'bout we discuss it over some phone records?"

She gave him an awkward look.

He winked and his lips curled mischievously.

The last car rolled out of the cemetery and Martinez got the feeling Brandon saw his vehicle. Not that he cared. The two of them sat in silence for a few minutes before they noticed a man walking towards the open hole in the ground that would soon be filled with dirt by cemetery employees.

"Looks like you may have called it, Detective. So, now what's your plan?"

"We'll just sit here and wait for him to leave. Before I can do anything, I need to identify him. We'll get close enough behind his vehicle to get his plate number so I can run it."

"I'm not sure that's the best way to go about it, do you?"

"Of course it is. What do you mean?"

"Well, what if it's not his car?"

He looked at her weird. "Why wouldn't he be driving his car, Liz?"

She shrugged her shoulders. "I don't know. Not every one has their own vehicle, I guess. Or a driver's license for that matter."

He contemplated her logic for a moment. Before he could respond, she opened the car door and began to get out. "Liz, what are you doing? Liz!" She shut the door behind her and began walking towards the man. "Damn it!" screamed Martinez as he slammed his hand on the steering wheel. Rather than chase after her, he decided to sit tight and see how it played out.

She slowly walked up to the grave and stood some distance behind the young man. His hands were stuffed in the front pockets of his Khakis. Not noticing her at first, he was sniffling, quietly. He jumped when he realized he wasn't alone. "Jesus, lady!"

"I'm so sorry, I didn't mean to interrupt."

Using his sleeve as a tissue, he cleared his face. "Don't worry about it. I'm done here." He turned away from her and began to walk away.

She stepped up a bit closer. "Wait! I'm so sorry. Did you know Pam? She and I were friends years ago. I wish I would have stayed in touch." She looked down and forced tears from her eyelids then reached into her bag for a tissue.

Shaking off his own grief, he stopped and walked over to her. He shook his curly bangs out of his eyes and they fell perfectly over his eyebrow. "Hey, I'm sorry. I'm just not really – I didn't want to come. Are you okay?"

Wiping her nose with her tissue, she said, "Yeah, I know what you mean." She laughed it off. "I literally waited for the family to leave before getting out of my car. I didn't want to be here either but I would feel terrible if I didn't say goodbye." She put her tissue in her pocket and offered her hand to him. "I'm Lisa. Lisa Swanson. Pam and I went to high school together."

Shaking her hand he said, "Damian. Damian Burk. Sorry, I'm just not much of a people person. That's why I waited in my car too. Don't really need the family drama, ya know?"

She rolled her eyes in agreement. "Yeah, right? So, how did you know Pam?"

"We worked together at Creative Industries." He starred down into the ground. "Such a talent gone to waste." Tears fell down his defined cheekbones. "I'm sorry." He began to walk way. "I'm really sorry, but I have to go." He wiped his nose and stuffed his hands back into his pants pockets before briskly walking back to his vehicle. He turned on the ignition, and quickly drove from the site leaving Elizabeth standing alone over Pam's grave.

Her eyes suspiciously followed Damian's vehicle until it was out of sight. Looking down at Pam's coffin covered in expensive flowers she said, "I'm so sorry this happened to you, Pam. I promise we'll find whoever did this."

Reaching Martinez's vehicle, she jumped into the passenger seat and closed the car door. Martinez gave her a scolding look.

"Damian Burk. They worked together at Creative Industries." She smiled being quite proud of herself.

His facial expression failed to change.

"What?" she asked befuddled by his irritation. "You're welcome."

THE SUN dimly shone through the second story windows of Brandon's lakeside apartment as he sat alone on his sofa. His tie hung loosely, half way down his unbuttoned white shirt, sleeves rolled up to his forearms and tucked in on one side of his black pants. He grabbed his rocks glass, taking the last sip of Johnnie Walker Black Label and chomping down on the ice cube, when there was a rap at the door. He ran his fingers through his disheveled hair and forced himself to get up and answer it.

Walking sluggishly into the foyer, he reached the door, unlocked the deadbolt, and slowly pulled it open. Sam stood on the other side with a concerned look on her face. He looked at her and said nothing.

Her blue eyes peered up at him from under her black bangs. Shrugging her shoulders she said, "I thought you could use some company." She lifted a brown bag in front of him and pulled out the bottle enough for him to see the black label. Opening the door a little more, he moved to the side to allow her entry.

She walked straight to the kitchen and set the bottle on the island. Brandon returned to his place on the sofa and she grabbed his glass to fill it for him. She opened a few cabinets before finding the rocks glasses and poured herself a drink as well before sitting next to him on the plush cushions.

Looking around for a moment she thought to herself how nice his place was. Large picture windows facing the lake, which allowed plenty of natural light to showcase the original brick; antiquated piping lined the corners of the walls and ceiling for a stylish, vintage feel against the new granite countertops and expensive tile and hard wood floors. After taking a sip of whiskey she asked, "So, how you holding up?"

Raising his glass he said, "Johnnie's doin' me right so far."

Grabbing her hair, she pulled it over her left shoulder. "I wanted to check on you but I also wanted to fill you in on what's going to appear in tomorrows run."

Rubbing the stress from his neck he said, "Please tell me he didn't..."

She set her glass down on the coffee table and placed her hands on his forearm. "Brandon, trust me. It's best if we get ahead of this. Jim did the right thing. He had me work the write up. Right now, you're the grieving husband, not suspect number one. Of course, according to

Silverton Police, her death is still under investigation and they are not willing to make a statement at this time. That only helps you." She reached in her bag and pulled out a paper, setting it on the table in front of him. "I brought it with me in case you wanted to read it."

He eyed the paper for a moment before picking it up and glancing over it. "That's a nice write up, Sam. I appreciate it. But it doesn't change the fact that they are looking at me for this. That damn cop showed up at the cemetery," he said handing it back to her.

Flinging her hair behind her back she said, "Yeah, well, I took care of that."

As his eyes welled with tears he took a hard breath in and slowly let it out. Sam put her drink down placing one hand on his knee and the other on his cheek, turning his face towards hers. "Hey – hey, hey... everything is gonna be alright, Brandon."

As he placed his hand on hers and looked into her eyes, she leaned forward and kissed him lightly on the lips. Stopping for a second to gauge the other's emotion, they latched onto each other in a sexual frenzy. Brandon pushed her onto her back and ripped open his shirt before unbuckling his belt and pulling down his pants. Sam lifted her dress over her head and flung it onto the floor. Her panties and bra followed.

Kissing his chest, she removed his shirt and grabbed him from behind, aligning their bodies. Once he entered her, they became imprisoned in a web of passion.

~

PEGGY WAS busy with a phone call when Elizabeth arrived, but she saw her pass by her door as she walked down the hallway. As soon as she hung up the phone she scurried to Elizabeth's office. No sooner had she sat in her chair, Peggy was standing in the doorway. "I need to see you in my office," she said sternly before quickly disappearing.

Rolling her eyes, Elizabeth pushed herself out of her chair and walked towards Peggy's office, passing China along the way. China gave her a look of indignation and Elizabeth took a deep breath before entering the dragon's lair. "Yes -"

"Shut the door and sit down."

Her eyes grew wide at Peggy's crudeness. "O-*kay...*"

As Elizabeth sat in one of the chairs across the desk, Peggy remained standing with both hands on her desktop. "I just got off the phone with Chief Holden." She cocked her head a little. "Would you like to tell me why you thought it was a good idea to show up at Pam DeFranco's funeral with Detective Martinez?"

Oh shit. Unsure of how to respond, she blurted out the first thing that came to her mind. "I really didn't think it was a good or bad idea to be honest."

"Bad idea. It was a bad idea, Liz."

She remained calm. "It's Elizabeth." *You are far from having earned that right, lady.*

Biting her bottom lip and then releasing it, she took a deep breath and continued as she looked down her nose,

"Eliza-*beth*, you are seriously out of line here. How *dare* you show up to the funeral of a victim! Do you know how bad that makes this office look?"

"I paid my respects to a woman I was trying to help, Peggy."

The color in her cheeks became a rose color. "Chief Holden received a complaint that Detective Martinez was 'staking out the funeral' with a blonde woman from the prosecutor's office. They found it offensive and intrusive and frankly, I couldn't agree more. There is a fine line, Elizabeth."

"Well *frankly*, Peggy, I find it somewhat suspect that someone even noticed that we were there. First of all, we were parked inconspicuously, far enough away that the average person in mourning wouldn't notice. And if they did, maybe it's because they had a guilty conscious."

"That is *not* for you or I to decide. You are not a detective, Elizabeth. Maybe we need to go over your job description? Or maybe you would feel more comfortable working for SPD rather than this office?" Her nostrils flared.

Rolling her eyes, Elizabeth felt defeated. She shook her head to the side and said, "Okay, I apologize, Peggy. At the time Martinez asked me I didn't see the harm. He was able to obtain a new suspect in the case with my help and, like I said, I paid my respects." She stood up to leave and added, "I should emphasize the fact that whoever made the call to Chief Holden, should be made aware to Martinez because I am sure the family of the victim would *never* have been concerned, least of all noticed." She grabbed the handle to the door and asked, "Can I get back to my work, please?"

Peering down her nose and frustrated with Elizabeth's lack of remorse and respect for authority, she waved her hand demanding Elizabeth's exit. "I'll be speaking with Marilyn about this."

Not responding, Elizabeth walked out the door and down the hall to her office. *Whatever Peggy. Cheese and rice!* She took a beeline to China's office, who was diligently working at her computer, and flung herself into the chair in the corner. She sighed deeply.

Jumping at the distraction, China laughed at herself and said, "Damn Liz! Give a girl a little warning next time, will ya?"

Brushing a few hairs out of her face she apologized. Then she took her voice down a few decibels. "You know, Peggy Cabot is the worst thing that has happened to this office since we've been here. What was it, two, three years we haven't had or needed a supervisor?"

China turned in her chair to give her full attention. "Two. It's been two years, honey."

"It's not that I'm completely opposed to having a supervisor per se, but what the hell? *This* is what we get stuck with? I swear, China, if she looks at me down her nose one more time – Oh my God, I can't even stand her nasally, pretentious voice! Like she is so much better than us. She has a BA. I have a frigin' law degree for crying out loud."

"Don't feel bad. She made a comment about my clothes today." She pursed her lips together and batted her eyes.

She eyed China up and down. She had on an off-white button-down shirt, a black pencil skirt hanging just a few inches above the knee, and a pair of black high heel open-toed shoes that wrapped around her ankles. Stunned, she asked, "What about your clothes?"

"Well, let's see, my skirt is too short, my top is too revealing, and I need to look a little more professional."

"Oh, come on? What the..."

Waving her French manicured nails in front of her she flung her bangs off her brows and said, "I kid you not. She literally asked me to button my shirt up further. As if it's *my* fault she has no cleavage. I have been working here how long? No one has ever made a comment about the way I dress. Hell, at least she kinda has a reason to be on you but I haven't done anything to warrant her riding my ass. Jealous bitch."

A little offended, Elizabeth replied, "I haven't *really* done anything, either."

"You know what I mean. I got one word for you, Liz. Cankles. And now we can add superiority complex to the mix. *Per*-fect combination." She frowned.

"I guess we should get something done before she comes down here and yells at us both."

China scrunched her eyebrows together and curled her lips. "Screw her. Peggy obviously has issues. She's pissed off because you're smarter than her and she hates the fact that I am ten times more attractive. I really wouldn't worry about it too much."

"Yeah, but still."

"Come on, Liz." Her shaped brow was high and rounded. Matter-of-factly she reminded her, "Doctor's wife." Changing the subject she asked, "So how was lunch with your Latin Lover anyway?"

"Okay I guess. Pam's boyfriend showed up after the family left just like Angel anticipated. I was able to get his name so he could run a background check on him."

Her face filled with excitement. "Success! You guys should open up your own PI business." It was like she had an epiphany. "Oh my God, Liz, that's it! Angel can be the detective, you be the lawyer, and I'll take care of the office. Win, win, win!"

"Really, China? That's crazy."

"Uh, not crazy, entrepreneurial. One of these days you're going to totally love one of my ideas and we're both going to leave all the Peggy Cabots in the world behind forever."

Elizabeth stood to leave. "Well, for right now, we should both get back to work before Jabba the Hutt makes her way down the hall and catches us."

"Hey, a girl can dream, right?"

CHAPTER 12

Exhausted after a long day, Elizabeth pulled down the gravel driveway to the lake house looking forward to a glass of wine and an evening with Martinez, even though he was bringing work with him. Grabbing her bag from the passenger seat she exited her vehicle and headed to the steps leading to the screened in porch when she heard a clanking noise. Cautiously, she crept to the door.

"Son of a bitch! You mother -"

"Uncle Bill! What on earth are you doing? You scared the crap outta me!" Entering the porch she ran to his aid. He was in the entry to the house, the door wide open, fiddling with something on the inside wall next to the door. His tools spread out all over the welcome mat.

"Hey baby girl! Grab me that Phillips-head, will ya? It fell over there in the corner somewhere."

Looking in the corner of the porch under a table

holding a potted plant, she found the screwdriver and handed it to him. "Honestly, Bill, what the hell are you doing?" Squeezing past him, she tossed her bag on the dining room table.

Grunting while he tightened the screws he said, "What I should have done before you ever moved back into this house." He moved away from the small white box secured to the wall. "Making sure you don't have any intruders. I'm a little too old to make it here as quickly as I need to if you have any trouble. This system here is gonna help both of us out." He wiped the sweat from his forehead with a cloth from his back pocket. "You got any cold beer in the fridge?"

Walking towards the kitchen she said, "You know, I really appreciate what you're trying to do here, but I don't think it's necessary." She pulled a couple beers out of the fridge and popped the tops off, handing one of the bottles to him.

Bill looked at it sideways. "What the hell is this? Corona?" He uttered a profanity under his breath before hesitantly taking a swig. "And I don't wanna hear no bullshit. I got a call from Martinez. Said we got a little problem on our hands with Robinson being released this week. I'm not taking any chances with that bastard." He handed her a piece of paper. "This is the code you enter to turn the alarm on and shut it off. It's your parent's anniversary. Figured it was the easiest number for you to remember. Better than your birthday, which I'm sure that asshole has branded into his sick head."

The sound of popping gravel stopped Elizabeth from arguing with him. She sighed deeply grabbing the piece of paper from him. Hearing footsteps come onto the porch they both walked out to meet Martinez.

Sticking out his right hand, Martinez said, "Good to see you again, Red."

He wiped his hand off on his beat up jeans before gripping Martinez's hand tightly. "How you doing, Son? Just finishing up with getting that security system in."

"Nice! Did it give you any trouble?"

Bill shook his head. "No trouble at all. Piece of cake."

Elizabeth studied Martinez intently and a shadow of flirtatious annoyance crossed her face. "So, I hear you had something to do with this?"

Bill guzzled down his beer and set the empty bottle on the wicker table. "Well, on that note, I think it's time for me to head home. Martinez, I'm sure you can show Liz how to use it?"

Nodding his head he said, "Of course." He looked at her and gave her a crooked smile.

"All right then," said Bill. Let's do dinner again real soon." He kissed Elizabeth on the cheek and whispered, "Go easy on 'im, kid. And get some real beer will ya?"

Bill walked out and shut the screen door behind him. Elizabeth curled her first finger and motioned for Martinez to follow her into the dining room. Hanging his head, he complied. He shut the door behind him and set his folder on the table. "Look, Liz..."

She put up her hand. "I don't wanna talk about it."

Thinking he was being let off easy, he sat down and pulled out the phone records. Elizabeth went to the living room and pulled out a couple albums, placing them strategically on the turntable in the order she wanted to hear them. Phil Collins began ringing through the room. She walked back into the dining room and sat at the head of the table. "So, what do we got?"

Sighing he said, "Alright, well, I got the phone records for Brandon and Pam for the previous few weeks prior to her death. I'm guessing they have something to tell us."

Grabbing her shoulder bag from the middle of the table, she pulled out a legal pad and a pen. Pushing her hair behind her left ear she said, "Okay, so, lets start from the beginning."

He sat back in the chair for a moment. "Just so you know, I'm sorry Peggy was brought into this.

She stopped herself from looking at the first page of records. "Actually, now that you bring it up, I wonder if I should even be helping you with this."

"Holden didn't really have a problem with us being there today. But he did say he was under an obligation to tell Peggy due to whoever made that call."

"Yeah, well, I'm already on her shit list. She seems to think I'm over stepping my boundaries." She pursed her lips and jerked her head a bit, her eyes rolling in the same direction.

"I'm sorry, Liz."

"It's not your fault. Honestly," she began lip-syncing to

the song playing in the background, 'I Don't Care Anymore.'

His lips curled into a devious smile. "For the record, I told Holden it was no different than if I took someone on a ride-along. He was cool about it. Said he was going to explain it to Marilyn the same way. I doubt *she* would have as big a problem with it as Peggy. I just told him what was up. I value your opinion, Liz, and sometimes you see things that the average person wouldn't see."

She scratched her head and smiled at his flattery. "Okay, so, as China would say, screw Peggy. Let's get on with it shall we?"

After thumbing through the pages for over an hour, studying the phone numbers and text messages, they managed to nail down five numbers that were regularly used. Two of the numbers consisted of Brandon and Pamela DeFranco. A third number was linked back to Jim West. Until further confirmation, one number that continuously called and texted Pam was assumed to belong to Damian Burk. The remaining number, linked to Brandon's phone, was set to the side for future reference.

Elizabeth rubbed her forehead to relieve the headache that was starting to form from the base of her neck. She looked at Martinez who was still studying a page from his stack. Her hand moved from her head to her shoulders, digging her fingers deep into her trapezius muscle to relieve the built up stress. She twisted her neck from side to side. "Are you hungry? Chinese sounds awesome right now."

Martinez sat back in his chair. "Yeah, we should probably take a break, huh?"

Getting up from the table, Elizabeth took a stack of menus out of the junk draw in the kitchen. "Okay, China Dragon it is. Do you prefer Chinese or Thai?"

"Both sound great. How 'bout we get a few dishes and share? As long as you get at least *one* meat dish for me. I don't wanna be starving in a couple hours."

She winked at him as she dialed a number from her phone. Once she had placed the order, she hung up and said, "Alright, should be here in 30 minutes or so."

Martinez stood up and placed his hands together behind his back to stretch his back and triceps. He sat back down and said, "Since we have a little time, there's something we should talk about."

She took a deep breath. "Come on," she said as she titled her head back. "Seriously?"

"Liz, it's not just gonna go away."

Becoming defensive she said, "Apparently not. Cheese and Rice! You were able to get my uncle over here to install a frigin' security system."

"He cares about you, Liz. And from what he told me, he wanted to do it long before you moved back in here."

"Not the point, Martinez." She circled the table. "God, half the time I feel like I have no control over any of these decisions, let alone being made aware they are even being contemplated."

He rested his head in shame. "I'm sorry. I should have

told you. I was afraid if I did, you would shut me down without hearing me out, just like you're doing now."

Guilt swept over her face. "I'm sorry. I'm not trying to shut you out. I just – Over the past couple years I just started to feel like I was in control of my life again, ya know? And you and Bill stepping in like this just feels like I'm losing control again. I don't wanna be a burden to anybody, Angel. I can take care of myself."

"I'm well aware of that, Liz. However, there are people who care about you and would do anything for you."

"Then please involve me next time. I lived for a long time feeling like I didn't have a choice. At least give me that."

"I'm sorry. I thought I was doing the right thing,"

"It's not that it's right or wrong, Angel. I appreciate it. I really do. But this is my house and my life. I think I should be the ultimate decision maker."

A wave of sympathy crossed his face. "I can understand that." Looking up from his shameful retreat, he asked, "So is this a bad time to bring up a protection order?"

"Seriously, Martinez?"

"Liz, he's getting out Friday. I'm just worried about you. Red's worried about you. China is worried about you! How is it that you, the one person truly affected, seem to have no concerns about this?"

"Of course I'm concerned. I'm just trying not to stress too much about it. For God's sake, if Steve Robinson wants to get to me, don't you think he will do just that?"

Martinez became stiff, his presence warrior-like. "We don't have to make it easy for him."

There was a knock at the door. Their food had arrived. Elizabeth grabbed her wallet from her bag and answered the door paying the man, tipping him generously. "Thank you so much!" Returning to the table she placed the bags in front of them.

Martinez began removing the small boxes of food from the bag and placing them on the table. "You know, you were wrong."

She became defensive. "Excuse me?"

"You don't need to place your address on a Civil Protection Order."

"What the hell are you talking about?"

"China told me why you didn't want to do the protection order. You don't need an address."

Elizabeth was growing more irritated. "Is that right?"

Finding the pepper steak and fried rice, he dug in with his chopsticks. His mouth full he said, "That's right, Miss Strong."

Grabbing the box of Shrimp lo mein, she said, "Do tell, Detective."

"I checked out the statute for a CPO. You only need to provide an address of where you want the defendant to keep himself from. Meaning, he doesn't know where you live. Therefore, no need to include it. He knows where you work, Liz. So you put your work address. That simple."

"That simple, huh? Do you even know what you're getting yourself into?"

Immediately after she asked the question, the Rolling Stones, Wild Horses, began playing on the stereo. Martinez put his chop sticks in his little white box and stood before her. He reached out his hand and she accepted. She put down her food and allowed him to pull her in close. As the song played, they swayed to the music. He whispered in her ear, "Wild horses couldn't drag me away."

As the song ended, they pulled away from each other and he kissed her lightly on the mouth. 'Can't You Hear Me Knockin' began to play. He looked deep into her blue eyes. "We're not trying to take your choice away, Liz. We're just trying to get ahead of the game and help."

"I get it." Her arms circled his neck. "Just make sure I'm a part of next time, will ya?"

His nose swiped across hers. He felt the warmth of her breath. "I'll always be here for you. I'm sorry if my protective side got away from me."

Shrugging her shoulders she gave in, "It's okay. I get it. Kind of." Pulling away, she sat back in her chair. "Anywho! Back to Pam DeFranco."

He sat down attempting to cover up the look of defeat on his face. "Absolutely. So. Here we are, the day of her death. There is a text message just like Brandon said. He received a text from Pam at 8:32 pm saying she was going to her sister's house."

Elizabeth studied the page in her hand. "That's the last

text sent from her phone. There's a bunch of missed calls after that. Looks like that was the last time she talked to anyone. However, before she sent the text to his phone, she received a text at 7:48 from his number asking her to meet him at their favorite place. But, I'm just curious why it reads differently than the rest of them."

"Really? Let me see that."

She got up, moved around the corner of the table, and stood next to him placing the paper in front of him. "Look," she said pointing her finger where she wanted him to read. "That's his number, right?"

Martinez glanced back and forth between the two phone records. "That's his number all right. Son of a bitch. He met her, they have a fight; he kills her and then sends the text to himself from her phone. The timing works. They meet at say eight o'clock, half an hour is plenty of time for him to take care of her, dump her body in the lake, and send a text. Then he tosses her phone in behind her. That's why we never found it."

"Not quite. Look at the number in brackets right below his."

The excitement in his voice dissipated. "Well what the hell does that mean?" He shoved the paper out of frustration.

Sitting back down in her chair, she replied, "I'm not sure really." She lifted her right foot and rested it on the seat before she began looking over the phone records again. "That's the first time that number pops up anywhere."

"For crying out loud. This case has been nothing but a dead end from the get go." He sat back and grabbed a take-out box plunging the chopsticks into the food, contemplating whether he could stomach another bite.

"Maybe not." She jumped up from her seat and went to the living room to fish for her laptop. Grabbing it from the end table she excitedly sat back down at the dining room table and opened the screen. She turned on the airport, opened Chrome, and began typing in the search box. "I once read an article on a third party app someone created that allowed you to text or call any one, from any phone number, and you could choose which number showed up on the recipients phone."

Curious, he asked, "What the hell are you talking about, Liz?"

Finding the article she became excited. "No, seriously..." She flipped the laptop around and set it in front of him. "Check it out."

Upon skimming through the article he said, "Well I'll be a son of a bitch."

"Exactly." She sat in her chair, proud of herself. "Find the owner of that number, and you find whoever lured Pam to the docks that night."

"And this is *exactly* why Peggy Cabot can go screw herself." He stood from his seated position and grabbed the arms of her chair, leaning over her possessively. "What do you say we take this in the other room?"

CHAPTER 13

The drive into the bureau Wednesday morning was sticky and Martinez couldn't wait to sit in the air-conditioning. After the previous day had been quite uneventful and full of paperwork, he was anxious for things to begin churning again. With Shawn out of the office for the day, he was hoping to quietly get some work done. He sat down at his computer and opened his email. The cell phone company returned his email regarding his request for the owner of the phone number found on Pam's phone record.

"Hot damn!" Quickly opening it in hopes of having a name, his excitement diminished when he read the number belonged to Marshal Media Corporation. Although they did confirm it was sent via a third party application that allows a person to send a text to any number with the allusion of coming from a specific contact. "For God's sake," he said as he shook his head from side to side. He looked at the phone number again. *I could just call the damn number. Nah, that would be a waste of time. No one would give me any information. Then again... Screw it.*

He picked up the receiver to his office phone and dialed the number. It rang a few times before going to voicemail with a generic recording. After hanging up the phone he moved on to his computer and went straight to Google to search when his office phone rang. "Detective Martinez."

"Hello, this is Damian Burk. You've been trying to contact me?"

"Mr. Burk! Yes, yes I have." Martinez fumbled around his desk for a pen and pad of paper. "Thank you for returning my call. I was hoping you could come down to the station to answer some questions regarding Pam DeFranco." Glancing over at the caller ID he wrote down the phone number Damian called from.

"I don't think so. You can ask me some questions, but now's your chance. Take it or leave it."

"Okay, let me start by asking how you knew Mrs. DeFranco?"

"We worked together at Creative Industries."

"Was your relationship strictly professional?'

"If your asking me that question, I assume you already know the answer."

"Look, Mr. Burk, I'm just trying to find out what happened to Pam. If you cared about her, I would think you would want to help in whatever way you could. Unless, of course, you have a guilty conscious."

There was a long pause and Damian sighed. "Pam and I worked together for about three years. We started seeing each other about a year ago."

"Did Mr. DeFranco know about the two of you?"

"She recently told him. I know he was pissed. She also found out she was pregnant not long ago."

"Did she tell her husband about the pregnancy?"

"I know she was planning on it. Whether or not she got around to it, I don't know."

"Do you know who the father was?"

"Pam told me it was mine. She said she hadn't slept with Brandon in a few months. Honestly, it didn't matter to me who the father was. Pam and I were going to raise the baby together. It was mine regardless of some stupid test."

"Mr. Burk, before Mrs. DeFranco told her husband about the affair, do you have any idea what kind of relationship they had?"

"I don't know, man. I only know what Pam told me. Brandon worked all the time. She said he was married to his work; he didn't want a wife let alone a child. She wasn't happy. I seemed to make her happy."

"Mr. Burk, did Mrs. DeFranco ever mention a Samantha Brown?"

"Pfft, yeah. I think she's the reason Pam and I got together in the first place. She suspected Brandon was having an affair with her but she could never prove it."

"Did you ever get the impression that Mr. and Mrs. DeFranco's marriage was in a volatile state?"

Damian's reaction to the question was a mix between a sigh and a laugh. "Pam was sleeping with me and Brandon was more than likely sleeping with Sam. What do *you* think?"

The reality of his answer struck Martinez to the core. He knew it was a stupid question, but one that had to be asked. "Mr. Burk, I do appreciate your time and your candidness. If I have any other questions, do you mind if I reach you at this number?"

"Look, man, I called you for Pam. I've told you everything I know. Just find the asshole responsible for this."

"Thank you, Mr. Burk. You have -"

Martinez looked at the receiver of his phone after he heard the click on the opposite end and took a breath. He hung up the phone and crosschecked the number on the caller ID to the number on Pam's phone records. It was confirmed to be Damian Burk. That didn't help him in the least to find out the mystery number that texted Pam's phone. He went back to the Internet to find out a little more about Marshal Media Corporation. After clicking on a few links he found what he was looking for.

Once again he picked up the receiver and dialed another number. After selecting a couple prompts, he finally reached a human. "Yes, hello. This is Detective Angel Martinez with the Silverton Police Department. I need to speak with Mr. Jim West, please."

"What's this regarding?"

"I'm afraid it's a personal matter."

"One moment please." Once the operator put him on hold, he heard a recording for the end of the summer festivities in down town Silverton.

Jim West answered on the opposite end. "Detective Martinez, good morning! What can I do for you this fine day?"

"Hello, Mr. West. I was hoping you could answer some questions for me regarding my investigation into the death of Pamela DeFranco."

"Well, Detective, I've been expecting a call from you for some time. You can ask as many questions as you like, however, I'm afraid each and every answer of mine will be to refer you to our legal department."

"You mean to tell me you refuse to answer some simple questions regarding policy at the Silverton Tribune?"

Jim laughed. "I'm not refusing to answer anything, Detective. I am simply referring you to our legal department."

Becoming frustrated, Martinez asked, "So let me get this straight, you're a 'journalist'; the first ones to cry you want to get to the truth of matters and blast them into the world for everyone to read about. And when it comes down to it, when it affects you, you decide to run from facts? You have no problem defaming SPD and any other public servant, but you haven't even written a single thing regarding this investigation or Mr. DeFranco's possible involvement. Do you really want to risk the integrity of your newspaper by not cooperating?"

Jim confidently replied, "Ah, and that is where you are mistaken. I believe we're a lot more alike than you wish to admit. In our work, we both get to the truth of certain matters following basic Constitutional principals. And that is the epitome of integrity. We also protect our own. I see no need to inform the public, yet, of anything regarding this investigation. And as far as I'm concerned, Brandon has given you a solid alibi and you have nothing showing he was involved. If you want to try and ruin the name of one of my top journalists, you're certainly not going to get any help from me if I'm not legally obliged. You do your job, I'll do mine. Good day, Detective."

His frustration turned to anger as he heard the headset of the phone clangor on the other end. Hanging up his receiver, he ran his fingers through his cropped hair and took a deep breath before rushing to draft a warrant aimed at the Silverton Tribune. With the information he had, the judge was sure to sign it and he vowed to personally deliver it to Jim West himself.

Warrant in hand, he made his way downstairs to the station. Officer Lucas was bringing a drug suspect in for processing, Martinez interrupting his path. "Hey, Lucas, you gotta minute?"

Lucas ordered his handcuffed suspect to the bench beside them. "Don't go anywhere." He winked sarcastically. Walking over to Martinez, he asked, "What's up?"

He lifted his chiseled chin questionably. "You find out

anything about our mystery Buick down at the docks or heard anything from Border Patrol?"

Lucas pursed his lips in a disappointing manner and shook his head. "Dead end. Border Patrol was in the middle of their shift change, so nothin' there. And the Buick belongs to a homeless guy. Parks down there some nights and moves his car periodically so we leave him alone. Even if he did see something, he ain't talking."

Patting him on the shoulder, he continued towards the Judge's chambers. "All right, man. Thanks."

CHINA HAD a long day at court and took a late lunch. When she arrived back at the office, she dropped her things on her desk and slid across the hall to see Elizabeth. Seating herself in one of the chairs across from the desk, she crossed her tan legs and gracefully placed her hands on her knees. "Sooo, my pretty. How was your little meeting with the Wicked Witch?"

Stopping her work at the computer, Elizabeth sat back and placed her arms on the branches of the chair. "It pretty much ended in a stalemate. But no monkeys were circling, so there's that. Peggy basically tried to tell Marilyn I was insubordinate for going to the funeral and Marilyn wasn't seeing it her way. I guess when Chief Holden called Marilyn about the complaint, he went to bat for me."

China's eyes glowed. "Wow, no kidding. I need me one

of those detective thingies!" She laughed out loud at her own comment.

Tilting her head she batted her lashes and flicked a lock of her hair flirtatiously, Elizabeth said, "Don't hate."

"I'm sure it would be a different story if you crashed the funeral or something." She shook her head out of frustration. "It's *not* that serious."

"I just don't get why Peggy is so hell-bent on trying to get me in trouble with Marilyn."

"I told you Liz, she's jealous. Plain and simple. You're a threat to her. We both are." She shrugged her shoulders.

"So where did you go after court anyway?"

Flexing her eyebrows, she gave Elizabeth a devious grin. "I had my own pretrial with a sexy defendant. Putting that man away for any amount of time, not being able to please a woman, should be a crime in itself."

Elizabeth scrunched her nose. "Eew. I think I need a shower now." She shuddered. "Okay, now that I have that thought out of my head."

"*What*? Just stating facts. Too bad I can't talk to the judge. Try and get him off, ya know?" She pulled a mirror from her purse and checked her lipstick. "Oh wait, I just did!" Laugher rumbled from the bottom of her belly.

Smiling, Elizabeth looked down and placed her forehead in her hand, shaking it from side to side. Glancing back up at China and giggling she said, "You need serious help. But I still love you. And actually I've decided to take some of *your* advice, believe it or not."

Her face turned from surprised to excited. "Really? You

decided to try that little trick I told you about with Martinez, didn't you?"

"No! I swear is that all you ever think about?"

She sat for a moment contemplating.

"Forget I asked." With a slight giggle, she put her hands up and redirected the conversation. "No, I decided to listen to you and Martinez and renew my CPO. He said he would hand deliver it to Steve himself. We're pretty sure I wouldn't have a problem getting it with the phone call and everything that went on with Johnnie Warren."

"Oh, I'm so glad, Liz! Look at *you*." She graciously placed her hand on her chest. "Taking advice from *me*." Becoming serious, she flung her bangs our of her eyes, crossed her hands back on her knees, and said, "I'm sure that Latin lover of yours plays a bigger role than I do. But, I'll take it. So, when do we go to court?"

"It will have to be today or tomorrow considering he's being released Friday. We just have to talk with Marilyn and let her know. And I'm sure she will want me to fill in Peggy and let her know what's going on, considering she's our 'superior' and all..."

CONFIDENTLY WALKING into the prosecutor's office lobby, Martinez smiled and waved at Andrea on the other side of the glass. She perked up when she saw him and hit the buzzer allowing him entry. Turning the corner, he leaned on the cabinet separating Andrea's desk from the hall. He smiled wide. "How's it going?"

"Hey, Martinez! How are you? If you're looking for Elizabeth, she's in her office," she offered as she cheerfully turned back to her computer screen.

"Hey, thanks, I'll get with her in a sec, but I was hoping Marilyn was in."

Stopping what she was doing again, Andrea turned to him and mashed her lips together. "Hmm. I'm not sure exactly. I heard the door earlier but feel free to go back."

Walking past the secretaries, Martinez offered his hellos. He stood at the threshold of Marilyn's office and tapped his knuckle on the door. She looked up from her scattered desk. "Hey kiddo. Whatcha got for me," she asked as she continued to look for something in the sea of papers.

He took a seat across from her and propped his right foot up on his opposite knee. "I think Brandon DeFranco is good for killing his wife."

She stopped shuffling papers and looked up at him. "Is that right?"

Excited at her response, he leaned over the desk and handed her a summary of his investigation to date. "I just wanted to run all this by you before I move forward. I still need to deliver the warrant to the Tribune, but I'm confident of the confirmation. And of course, Holden wants me to bring him in for questioning one more time, see if we can get any more info out of him."

She studied the documents in her hand. "Seems to be

in order. It's circumstantial but I've gotten convictions on less. What do you make of the girlfriend?"

He rubbed his five o'clock shadow. "Well, she *is* his alibi. She could be lying to protect him. She could be involved. I'm going to try and bring them both in at the same time, pin them against each other if possible."

Pulling off her glasses, she placed the end of the frame between her teeth and wrapped her thin lips around it. Twisting her chair back and forth a couple times, she said, "See if you can get anything out of them. I mean, the more we have the better, of course. But I think I'm comfortable with what you have here."

Nodding his head, he said, "Alright. That's all I needed. I'll get the warrant served this afternoon."

She smiled and winked at him. "Good work, Detective." She put her glasses back on and returned to her paperwork.

"Thank you, Marilyn." He started to step out of her office and turned back around. "Hey, is it okay if I stop back and see Liz before I go?"

She looked up over her frames at him. "About that. You know it doesn't bother me about you and Elizabeth helping each other. I mean we're both on the same team here. Just remember, I'm not the only person she reports to now."

He sucked in his bottom lip and bit down hard before nodding at her again. "Copy that."

Walking back through the main office, he smiled at all the secretaries and headed down the hall to Elizabeth's office. As he approached, he heard Elizabeth and China laughing. Leaning into the doorway, he said, "Now ladies, it sounds like we are having *way* too much fun in here."

Perking up in her chair, Elizabeth's face lit up. "Hey, you!"

He looked at her possessively but lovingly. "Hey, yourself." He moved his eyes to China. "Hey, China. How's it goin'?"

Seeing that as her cue to leave, China picked up her things and walked past him, giving him sexy eyes. "Hey Martinez..." She turned back to Elizabeth and winked at her. "You kids behave now."

Taking the seat that China occupied, he made himself comfortable. "So how's your day going, Bella?"

She smirked and rolled her eyes. "It's going, I guess. Good to see your smiling face though!"

"Well, maybe I can make it a little better for ya."

Her face was speculative and she giggled out loud. "Well you can certainly try."

He sat back in the chair with confidence. "I just spoke with Marilyn about my investigation on Pam DeFranco's death and I'm pretty sure I should be making an arrest before the weekend."

"Really? Well I guess that is some good news for a change."

He pulled the warrant out of his pocket and waved it in front of her. "Yep. I just need to deliver this warrant to Jim West's smug ass and solidify my suspicion. After I get what I need, I'll bring in Brandon DeFranco and his little girlfriend one last time, try and get one or both of them to give me something. Regardless, I'll have enough for an arrest."

A confused look swept across her face. "You know, I'm not a huge fan of the Tribune either, but it seems like you take it a little personal. I mean, don't get me wrong, I took some of their articles a little personal myself but..."

Leaning forward he attempted to defend his stance. "I don't have a problem with freedom of speech, Liz. What I do have a problem with is trying to protect someone who is guilty behind some Constitutional bullshit." He proceeded to tell her about his last conversation with Jim.

The look on her face was sympathetic. "Angel, I understand where you are coming from, but to be honest, I understand his side as well. He's not obligated to share anything with you. But that's why you have that warrant in your hand. You can't blame him for making you take the proper legal steps to get what you want, can you? He's right, you know. But so are you."

A little put off, he thought for a moment. "I get what you're saying. But Jim West is a smug asshole. I can't wait to deliver this."

Tilting her head in a compassionate manner, she said, "I want Brandon DeFranco as much as you do, but, I don't know, I guess we both need to put things in proper prospective when it comes to the Tribune. If it's not Jim West and Brandon DeFranco spewing their hate of SPD and the prosecutor's office, you know it would be someone else." She shrugged her shoulders.

He sighed. "Yeah, you got a point. But it's still gonna feel damn good setting this on his desk and bringing Brandon down."

"I get it. So, how 'bout I give you a little piece of information from my arsenal?"

He perked up. "Oh yeah? Whatchu got, Strong?"

"Interestingly enough, Pam's sister, Janet Burrows, called me after lunch. Said she received some mail for Pam at her house. From a divorce attorney."

He smirked. "So, she was seeking a divorce? Classic," he said as he shook his head.

She smacked her lips as she spoke. "Yeah, it appears so. Are we surprised?" she asked sarcastically.

"Not in the least. It also comes as no surprise it's officially a homicide. Dr. Wexler emailed me the autopsy report confirming the cause of death. He also confirmed she was pregnant."

Sadness washed over her face. "Oh my God, seriously?"

"Yeah, I know, right? Hopefully, once I nail this bastard, Marilyn will authorize two murder charges."

She sighed. "Hopefully." There was a silent pause. Elizabeth tried to push the visuals out of her head. "Hey, can you do me a favor?"

"Of course, Liz. Anything."

"Can you let me know as soon as an arrest is made and let me tell the family? I've been working pretty close with Janet. I would really like to be the one to tell her."

"I can absolutely do that." He stood up to head out.

Standing with him, Elizabeth had one more request.

"Hey, I know your busy today, but I was hoping you were free tomorrow afternoon, say after lunch?"

"I don't have anything going on so far, unless of course I can get Brandon in again for questioning. Why, what's up?"

She took a deep breath. "Well, China and I are going over to court. I have my petition for a CPO filled out and I'm ready to request it from the judge."

His face showed signs of shock and relief as he steadied himself against the doorframe. "Wow. Okay. Of course, I'll be there. Just say the word. I'll be sure to clear my calendar after lunch."

Stepping toward him, she placed her hand on his arm and looked up into his brown eyes. "Thanks."

He gently took hold of her chin with his thumb and his forefinger. "I'll call you later, k?"

Smiling as she nodded, her eyes didn't leave him as he walked down the hall and out the door.

CHAPTER 14

Brandon arrived at the Tribune early Thursday morning. He was dressed for work in a light blue and white-checkered shirt and khakis. Reaching Jim's office, he rapped on the door and smiled. Jim, however, did not appear to be happy to see him.

"What are you doing here, Brandon? You're supposed to be on bereavement until next week."

Shutting the door behind him, he took a seat across from Jim. "I know, I know, but I can't just sit around, Jim. It's driving me nuts." He tossed a flash drive on the desk. "I finished the article series I told you about."

Sighing and shaking his head, he looked Brandon in the eyes. "There isn't going to be any series. I'm sorry, Brandon."

Looking confused and shocked, Brandon questioned his authority. "What the hell are you talking about? Jim, I've been working on this for weeks, man! The public has a right to this information. SPD and the prosecutor's office over step their bounds daily. Don't you think enough is enough?"

"Now is not the time for this, my friend. You are under investigation, for killing your wife!"

Standing up, Brandon continued his defense. "Really, Jim? After all these years you don't trust me? I've done the research. I now have personal experience and you're not gonna let me run with this? For God's sake, you haven't even come to my defense by conducting any kind of write up on the investigation at all. Frankly, I'm a little surprised."

Jim stood in response to Brandon's aggressiveness and placed his hands in front of him on his desk. "You're right, I haven't come to your defense at all. Detective Martinez has already contacted me fishing for information. And in my opinion, as Senior Editor, it is not in your best interest or the interest of the Tribune to even touch pen to paper on your wife's death. I trust you, Brandon, but you have to trust me as well. There is no comment from SPD on their investigation, only questions. Questions I am not willing to answer short of being legally obligated to do so. So at this point, you need to let this personal vendetta of yours go. End of discussion."

Brandon wasn't defeated just yet. "This is hardly a personal vendetta, Jim. I've been working on this for a while. You gave me the clearance when I presented you my proposal months ago. You can't yank this from me now. I need this. I need to work; it's all I have left. Jim, please..." he asked beggingly.

Sitting back down in his chair, Jim sighed and grabbed his chin, rubbing it while he thought. He placed his hands together and rubbed them slowly. "Alright, this is what we're going to do. Come back to work. Who am I to say what's best for you or how you should handle all of this. However, I'm still not running the series -"

"But Ji-"

Placing his hand up in a stop motion, Jim continued. "Once the smoke clears, and Detective Martinez is off your ass, I'll reconsider. That's final, Brandon." He looked in his eyes making sure his instructions resonated.

Although not happy, Brandon nodded his head and retreated to his office. Jim sat back and rubbed the stress from the back of his head. Not a minute later he heard a rap on his door. Martinez stood there with a smug grin on his face. The girl from the front desk popped up from behind him.

"Jim, I'm so sorry. I tried to stop him..."

"It's alright, Miranda. I'll handle this."

As she turned to head down the hall Jim looked at Martinez as he sat down. "What do you want, Detective? This is beginning to border harassment."

Martinez made himself comfortable in a chair on the other side of Jim's large executive desk and tossed the warrant on top so it slid across the smooth wood finish. Lifting his chin he said, "There's your warrant, Mr. West. It's pretty limited and self-explanatory. If you don't mind,

I'll just sit here and wait while you gather the info I need." He winked.

Opening up the warrant Jim began to read it. Shaking his head he sighed. "I don't understand this."

Martinez rolled his eyes to himself. "I need confirmation that the listed phone number belongs to this newspaper and a list of all individuals who have access to it."

Brandon came walking into the office with his head down, proofing an article. "Hey, Jim, I got a question for y-" As he looked up he was shocked and then confused. "What's going on, Jim?"

Standing to greet him, Martinez smiled. "Mr. DeFranco, just the man I wanted to see."

"Brandon, I think maybe you should go home for the day and let me handle this."

Before he could respond, Martinez said, "Oh no, I think Mr. DeFranco would have plenty to add to the conversation. Matter of fact, we could just go down to the station and straighten all this out right now."

"Jim, what is he talking about?" His eyes moved from Jim to Martinez and back to Jim.

"He has a warrant, Brandon."

"A warrant? For *what* exactly?"

Jim didn't take his eyes off of him. They screamed at him to take his advice. "Brandon, please go home and let me handle this."

Martinez chimed in again. "You know, I also received the autopsy report from Dr. Wexler on the cause of your wife's death." He shrugged his shoulders and sighed.

"Unfortunately, I left it at my office. How 'bout you follow me down there and I can go over that with you as well? Figure all this out."

Confidence filled Brandon's chest as he inhaled deeply. "You know what, Detective? Let's go."

"Brandon, you don't know what you're doing-"

"No, Jim. I know exactly what I am doing. This is bull- shit and I've had enough!" Pulling his keys from the front pocket of his Khakis he said, "I'll be back in a while."

His eyebrows shooting up with excitement and surprise, Martinez followed Brandon out. He turned back to Jim as if he won. "I guess he'll be back in a while, Mr. West."

As soon as they were out of earshot, Jim slammed his hands on the desk. "Son of a bitch!"

Sam stood at the entryway of his office with a folder cradled in her arms, flinching at the tone in his voice. "O- kaaay. What did I miss?"

Looking at her with his ice-blue eyes he begged, "Please follow Brandon down to the station. Make sure he doesn't say or do anything stupid."

Her jaw dropped as her forehead wrinkled. "What the hell is he going to the station for?"

Jim tilted his head and stretched his neck from side to side. "Detective Martinez was here with a warrant. Also said he had the autopsy report. It's not looking good, Sam. And Brandon is at his wits end; exactly where Detective Martinez wants him. He set the bait and reeled him right in. Just please go supervise."

"Of course." Without hesitation Sam returned to her office, dropped her files on the desk, grabbed her purse, and ran out of the Tribune to try and catch up to them.

She ran up to Brandon's vehicle and grabbed the handle just before he shut the driver's side door. Catching her breath she pleaded with him. "Brandon, what are you doing?"

Turning on the ignition, he paused. "Sam, please don't. I'm taking care of this once and for all." Looking into her eyes he grabbed the handle from inside. "Please let go."

She flipped her long black hair behind her shoulder and met his gaze with sincerity. "I'm not trying to stop you, Brandon. But I'm begging you to at least let me come with you. You're doing exactly what Detective Martinez wants you to do and this can't end well."

He placed both hands on the steering wheel and leaned his head against the headrest, sighing and closing his eyes for a moment. Leaning forward he put the car in reverse to back out. "Fine. Get in."

Martinez was well ahead of them as they pulled out of the Tribune parking lot. Making it to SPD headquarters, they pulled into a visitor parking spot. Sam's eyelashes blinked from under her bangs. "You know you don't have to do this."

Without giving it another thought, Brandon angrily opened his car door and said, "Yes I do." Slamming it behind him, he sprinted up to the glass doors entering the station with Sam quickly following behind. The lobby being empty, Brandon approached the records window.

There was a lady at the desk a few feet away. When she failed to acknowledge his presence, he knocked on the glass. "Excuse me?"

Her eyes rudely glanced up at him before she turned her gaze back to her computer screen.

He knocked on the window again. "Excuse me? I'm here to see Detective Martinez. He just came in minutes before me."

Taking her time to finish whatever she was working on, she finally rose out of her seat and came to the window. In a non-urgent manner she replied, "I'm sorry. Can I help you?"

Growing irritated, Brandon kept his composure. "I'm here to see Detective Martinez. He has information about my wife's death."

The clerk looked at him over the top of her glasses. "Do you have an appointment?"

Sam stood next to Brandon with her arms crossed, growing more pissed off by the moment. Before he could answer, she responded, "Yes! He's expected. Please let him know Mr. DeFranco has arrived."

Looking crossed, the clerk said, "Sure thing," and returned to her desk, picking up the phone receiver. Before she could dial a number, Martinez sprung from the heavy steel door leading from the bureau stairs to the lobby.

"Mr. DeFranco, thank you for coming." He motioned to the clerk and then turned his attention to Brandon and Sam. "Ms. Brown. I'm sorry, I wasn't expecting you."

Sam pursed her bright red lips. "I'm sure you weren't."

A tad perturbed, Martinez led Brandon into the interview room. He stopped Sam before entering. "If it's alright with you, I have some intimate details of the investigation I need to share with Mr. DeFranco alone."

Without saying a word, she turned to Brandon for guidance.

"Detective, I'm sure nothing you have to say can offend my colleague. I'd rather have her join us, if it's all the same to you."

Shrugging his shoulders he thought to himself, *Two for one special today. Hot damn!* "Alright then." He motioned Sam to enter and have a seat next to Brandon as he sat in the chair across from them and gently set a file folder on the table. Opening the file he pulled out the autopsy report. "So, I guess we can start with Dr. Wexler's initial findings." He spread out a couple documents in front of them. His eyes focused on Brandon as he spoke, gauging his reaction. "It's been confirmed that your wife was indeed the victim of foul play. She suffered a harsh contusion to the head that knocked her unconscious but the actual cause of death was due to drowning."

As Brandon read the report, Sam reached over and grabbed his hand in support. Shaking his head he tried to vocalize his amazement. Placing the report back on the table in front of him he responded, "I'm at a loss for words here, Detective. Who would do something like this?"

Relaxing back in his chair, Martinez glanced back and

forth between the two of them. "That's what I was hoping you could help *me* with."

Brandon leaned his elbows on the table and began rubbing his forehead with the balls of his fingertips. His hands fell in front of him. "Look, it's like I told you, Pam didn't have any enemies. None of this makes sense to me."

Grinning inside, Martinez made his move. "Okay, maybe this will help." He reached into the file and pulled out the phone records. "You say on the night she was killed, Mrs. DeFranco sent you a text at around 8:30 PM, said she was going to stay with her sister for a few days?"

"That is correct."

"Right, so if you look on your phone records, you can obviously see that text." Pulling out another sheet of paper from his file he continued, "If you'll notice on Mrs. DeFranco's phone records, at 7:48 PM, your wife received a text from a number, that appears to be yours, asking her to meet you at your favorite place. Does your favorite place happen to be down at the docks, Mr. DeFranco?"

Shooting Martinez a look of disapproval, Sam quickly interjected. "Don't answer that Brandon."

Feeling empowered, Martinez shot back at her. "I'm sorry, Miss Brown, are you here for moral support or did you become a licensed attorney in the past week?"

Brandon appeared to be becoming more uncomfortable by the minute. He shoved the papers across the table. "Alright, what the hell is going on here?"

Sam stood from her seated position, her cheeks growing slightly red. "That's what I would like to know. Is

Brandon being detained or is he free to leave? Brandon, I think it's time for us to leave."

Anger took over his confused state. "No, wait a second, here. What are you saying, Detective? That I sent my wife a text asking her to meet me at the docks the night she died?"

Martinez was happy to have his attention. "It certainly appears that way at first glance." He took hold of the phone record and placed it in front of Brandon pointing as he explained. "The text actually came from this number here. It was sent via a third party application to make the receiver believe it was sent from your phone. Funny thing is, it was sent from a phone that belongs to the Tribune."

Brandon stood up and began to pace in the small room. "I'm afraid I have no idea what you're talking about." He leaned over the table and looked Martinez straight in his face. "I did *not* kill my wife!"

Allowing the moment to unfold, Martinez sat back and watched without saying anything. He saw the sweat forming on Brandon's forehead and Sam's nervousness forced her to stand in an attempt to calm Brandon down. She begged him, "Please, Brandon, it's time to go…" As she placed her hand on his forearm he forcefully pushed her away.

"No! Enough of this!" Shutting his eyes he took a deep breath before sitting back down and glancing at the phone records again. "What do you mean, the text was sent from a third party app?"

Excited to explain it to him, Martinez leaned forward.

"You see this number here? This is the number that actually sent the text to your wife's phone. However, an app was downloaded onto that phone that allows the user to call or text any other number in disguise. Meaning, I can use the app right now to call your phone and make it appear to be your wife calling you. Or Sam. Or any other number I choose."

Pulling out another piece of paper from his arsenal, Martinez said, "You know, not only was your wife murdered, she was pregnant at the time of her death."

Sinking back into her chair, Sam grabbed her mouth with her hands and muttered, "Oh my God."

Brandon did a double take. "She was *what?*"

His face grim, Martinez shook his head affirmatively. "I'm sure you were aware your wife was cheating on you, right? Was it yours or his? Do you even know?"

In fight or flight mode, Brandon chose to fight. "You know, I had no idea Pam was pregnant." His head shook from side to side and a tear formed in the corner of his eye. "But I knew about Damian Burk. That's what we were arguing about the night I was bogusly charged with domestic violence. Pam and I were already talking about divorce. That night solidified it. And then when SPD got involved, I made Pam a deal. She would help me with my article series, and I would sign the papers."

Sam looked at him in terror. "Brandon, what the hell are you saying?"

Feeling ashamed, he explained himself. "Look, Pam and I had not been getting along for a while. I was hurt when I found out about Damian." He looked at Martinez and stated absolutely, "But it didn't make me want to *kill* her." He paused for a moment. "I had an important article series about local law enforcement."

Martinez rolled his eyes and curled the corner of his lips.

Brandon stopped and glanced at him. "No offense. It's just business." Turning back to his story he said, "I was working on it for months. Jim had everything approved. When SPD got involved in my life, it almost seemed to good to be true. I decided I would wrap up the series with my own personal experience. Pam agreed to help me. Figured she at least owed me that." He sat back confident in his explanation of the chain of events. He turned his attention back to Martinez. "Hell, you guys already had me pegged as a wife beater, why on earth would I kill her?"

Sam looked up to the ceiling of the small room shaking her head as she defensively placed her arms across her breasts and took a deep breath attempting to hide the worry in her face.

His handsome face stern and filled with doubt, Martinez caught on to her body language, placed his strong forearms onto the table and crossed his fingers together. He starred Brandon down and said, "You know, that's quite a story there Mr. DeFranco. I'm afraid it just doesn't wash for me. See, I just delivered a warrant to your editor at the Tribune. Soon I'm going to have the phone records to the number I shared with you. There is no doubt the text your wife received luring her to the docks the night she was killed came from that phone.

"So, either *you* sent your wife the text from that phone in an attempt to cover it up, or someone else from the Tribune having access to that phone sent it. Again, in an attempt to cover it up."

Quickly rising from her seat, Sam spoke up. "Okay Brandon, I really think it's time for us to go. This is getting ridiculous."

After eyeing her up and down, Martinez kept his poker face and turned his eyes back to Brandon.

Meeting his gaze with a look of confusion, the wrinkles in Brandon's forehead began to diminish as the pieces fell into place for him. His squinted eyes turned to Sam and looked up to her, dumbfounded. "It was you."

Her heart began to pound beneath her firm chest. She grabbed her bag from the back of the chair and swung it around her shoulder. "I said it's time to go Brandon." She pushed in her chair and shot her eyes at Martinez defensively. "You're a real piece of work, Detective."

Brandon stood up and blocked her from leaving. "You crazy bitch. This whole time it was *you*."

Guilt washed over her. "Brandon, you don't know what you're saying."

He began backing her into the corner. "I'm afraid I know exactly what I'm saying. *You* came up with my alibi. *You* begged me to go along with you. That wasn't for my protection." Poking his finger into her chest, he declared,

"It was for your own. Wasn't it, Sam? For God's sake, you seduced me on the day of her funeral!"

Standing out of preparation for the fallout, Martinez put his hand on his weapon but he didn't interfere.

Fear washed over her face as he towered over her. She batted her long, thick lashes at him as she looked up into his fierce eyes. "Brandon, please don't let him fill your head with this bullshit!"

Without taking his eyes off of her, Brandon stood nose to nose with her and stated confidently, "Detective, I'm sorry I lied to you about my alibi. I'm also sorry I didn't see this all before. I wasn't with Sam. I was home alone. I got home that night around seven thirty. Pam was already gone. And then I got her text saying she would be at her sisters. That's all I know." The relief permeated from his breath.

Grabbing her chest trying to breath, Sam finally broke and screamed at him, "You *stupid* son of a bitch! She didn't deserve you!" She smacked him across the face and met his shock with malevolence in her gaze. "I sent Pam that text. I met her down at the docks and told her what a worthless, piece of shit wife she was. I followed her and Damian for months while you sat around and gave two shits. She couldn't even admit what a whore she was. Kept telling me it was none of my business and pushing me to get out of her way. And now she can rot in hell!"

Brandon grabbed Sam's flailing arms trying to stave off the attack. Martinez quickly circled the table, managing to get her hands behind her so he could cuff her. As he secured the handcuffs, Brandon slid against the wall to the other side of the room, bewildered, as she was escorted out.

Martinez walked her out of the interview room towards the station door as he recited the charges against her. "Miss Samantha Brown, you're under arrest for assault. You're also under arrest for the murder of Pamela DeFranco. You have the right to remain silent..."

Every extremity of Brandon's was frozen. He stood against the wall as she screamed back to him, "I sacrificed *everything* for you!"

Martinez led Sam through the door and down the hall to the first available holding cell. Removing the cuffs from her and shutting the cell door behind him he looked at her frail frame and shook his head in disbelief. "Sit tight. You've got nothing but time now."

Sam wrung her wrists as if the cuffs were too tight and she glared in his direction, her under eyes smeared with mascara. Sitting down on the metal bench she grunted, "I need to make a phone call." He walked away without responding. She jumped up from her seated position and ran to the cell bars, grabbing onto them with both of her hands. "I need to make a phone call!"

He continued walking away. When he reached the door to the lobby he heard an ear-piercing scream. Attempting to ignore it, he returned to the interview room. Brandon was sitting at the table with his head in his hands. "Mr. DeFranco?" He looked up, disoriented. His face was flush and his eyes appeared red. Sitting down across from him, Martinez was sincere. "I'm sorry, Mr. DeFranco. I don't think either one of us was expecting that."

Masking his inner turmoil with a deceptive calmness Brandon asked, "Am I okay to leave?"

Understanding he needed some time after the unfolding of recent events, Martinez nodded to him. "I hope you realize I'm going to need you to answer some questions in the near future."

Before walking out the door, Brandon turned to him. "I can't believe I'm saying this, but you'll have my full cooperation."

Reaching into his pocket to grab his phone, Martinez dialed Elizabeth. She answered immediately. "Hola, guapo."

He grinned from ear to ear. "Aye, me Beleza Blanca. I have news for you."

"Let me guess; you're waiting naked for me with wine and pizza?"

"Oh how I wish! I got one better for ya. Well, kinda. I made an arrest in Pam DeFranco's murder."

"Wow, seriously?"

"Serious as a heart attack baby doll. Samantha Brown is being processed as we speak," he said proudly. "You can go ahead and call the family. Let them know we still have some unanswered questions, so they can be filled in on all the details beginning of next week. But the arraignment should be first thing tomorrow morning."

Her voice showed her bewilderment. "Samantha Brown? Wha-aat?"

"Yeah, crazy story. I'll tell you all about it tonight over wine and pizza?"

"Yummy. I can't wait. You're meeting me and China at the courthouse later this afternoon right?"

"Four o'clock, right? I'll be waiting for you." His voice turned seductive. "Then after that, we can head to your house and get down to real business."

"Bring your handcuffs, Detective."

His eyes brightened and his eyebrows nearly touched his hairline. "¡Ay, caramba! No hay problema, seniorita."

ELIZABETH PUSHED the foam container to the other side of the picnic table and grabbed her belly. "Oh my God. I can't believe you talked me into eating that. Those were the best BBQ ribs I've ever had in my life. I think I'm going to vomit; I ate too much."

He smiled at her satisfaction. "At least it's Friday and you don't have too much time left at the office. Just make sure you rest up before tonight." Biting his bottom lip he smiled.

Flickering her eyebrows at him she assured him, "My nap is already planned." She looked around the park before turning her gaze to the lake in front of them. "I never even knew this little gem was here."

Taking the last bite of coleslaw, he closed the lid on

his container and wiped his mouth with his napkin. Well, it used to be until the city kicked him out for not having a permit. I had to call in a favor for a friend." Hearing footsteps on the grass behind them, Martinez turned around to see Miles approaching. "Speak of the dirty devil."

"Sup, Martinez?" He stood there with his hands in the pockets of his baggy jean shorts, his Dallas Cowboy's jersey hanging loosely over them. "I guess white folk like BBQ after all?"

Standing to greet him properly, Martinez said. "Indeed, my friend," and solidified it with a fist pump. He turned to Elizabeth introducing her. "Miles, this is Elizabeth Strong. Liz, I give you Miles Murphy."

Stroking his chin and nodding his head while he grinned, he looked her up and down. "That's what's up, lil' sista."

Martinez scowled and clenched his teeth causing his cheek to twitch.

Stepping back Miles dropped his hand from his chin. "Oooh, it's like that? I gotchu. My o-po-lo-gies." He offered his fist. "Nice-to-meet-you, Miss-*Strong.*"

Elizabeth giggled and pumped his fist. "It's nice to meet you, Miles."

He dropped his hand and began waving it in front of him. "Hey now, I'm the Medicine Man. Whatever your ailment-"

With censure in his tone, Martinez quickly corrected him. "It's Miles, Liz. Just Miles."

Backing up, he understood. "I gotchu, okay. I'm just gon' wait over here."

Giving him a nod, Martinez told Elizabeth, "I gotta take care of this and then I have to head out to Mansfield. I'm glad the arraignment went well this morning. Now you can take a little break." He grabbed her hand.

Letting a deep breath out, she had an air of calm and confidence, which he liked. "Sort of. Next week I need to begin preparing the family for trial."

"For right now just chill" His tone had a degree of warmth and concern. "You know, I am really proud of you for going to court yesterday and how well you handled yourself. You did the right thing."

Her eyes like sapphire, peered up at him. "Thank you for lunch. For *everything.*"

Kissing her on the forehead, he promised, "We'll pick this up later tonight. Okay?" Then he watched her as she left.

Miles walked up next to him. "Da-yum! Marti-*nez*, you da *man.*"

Scratching his five-o'clock shadow he said, "Watch it, Miles." The two of them continued to watch Elizabeth walk to her car across the street. She turned back, her blonde hair gleaming in the sun. She smiled at them and waved. "Wave to her, Miles." He obliged with an out of character, Steve Urkle smile and wave. Once she was in her car, Martinez asked him, "What do you got for me?"

"Ma-aaaan this shit be tight! I ain't even playin' wit you." He planted his fist in the palm of his other hand.

Frustrated, Martinez placed his hands in his front pockets, tilted his head in disbelief and said, "Come on, Miles."

"Look, bro, I'm serious. You know how hard it is to find a mole?" His arms moved in waves as he explained. "You start goin' down one tunnel and it jus' lead to another. This shit go wa-aay back. But my sources tell me, it started somewheres in the county's beloved drug-*task-force*." His tone and facial expression set off an alarm.

Martinez stiffened and shifted his mahogany eyes to Miles.

Tightening his lips together, he muttered, "Mmm hmm. Ima need some time." Walking away from Martinez, Miles turned his attention away from him to avoid a fall-out. "Ay, yo, Mr. Henry!" He pointed at Martinez. "You owe him a lunch, my man!" Then he strutted to his tricked out Cadillac, without giving Martinez a second glance.

ARRIVING in Mansfield just after two o'clock, Martinez rolled onto the prison grounds. He checked in with the guard, who directed him to the release gate. Circling around the prison, he drove down the long road to the gate and parked off to the side, waiting as he repeatedly checked his dash for the time. Within ten minutes, he heard the sound of the alarm indicating the oversized double steel door to the prison was opening. "Right on time," he said aloud to himself. He exited the vehicle and stood on the passenger side, leaning against the door and propping one foot up under his butt with his arms crossed, his chest protruding overtop of them.

A guard stood on either side as one of them gave directions to the prisoner standing in between them. A military green colored bag was strapped around his shoulder. He walked forward until ordered to halt. The guards walked to meet him a few feet from behind before the steel doors shut behind them. Again, the guard gave him instructions. He pushed a red button the size of his hand and the huge fenced gate lined with barbed wire clanged open as the one syllable alarm sound again.

Once the gate was fully opened, the guard ordered him to step to the yellow line three feet in front of him and remain there until advised he was no longer under the instruction of Mansfield Corrections. After the alarm sounded again, the gate closed behind him and the guard said, "Inmate number 34621, you are no longer under the control of Mansfield Correctional. You are free to leave the premises and reminded to report to your parole officer within 72 hours of your departure." And the guards proceeded back to the double steel doors entering the prison.

Using his foot to push himself away from the vehicle, Martinez dressed in his blue polo and jeans, his badge gleaming from his black belt, stately walked towards the prisoner. Once he was two feet within his reach, he tapped an envelope in his hand as he said, "Well, well, well.

Don't know how you did it, but you did it. Gotta hand it to you Robinson, you're smarter than you look."

Steve was clean-shaven, dark hair cropped short enough to leave his curls, and dressed in a silky black shirt with grey dress slacks. He slightly titled his head back, thickening the muscles in his neck, glaring down his nose at Martinez. "You here for a reason?"

Pulling his standard issue Oakleys off his face, he met Steve's gaze with authority. "You're bag doesn't really match your outfit, Robinson. You have plans tonight?"

"Matter of fact, I do. Been a *long* six years. I have some catching up to do. So unless you're here to give me a ride..." Before he could finish, a black four-door BMW with custom wheels slowly inched towards them.

Tipping the envelope towards him, Martinez waited for Steve to grab it and said, "Mr. Steven Robinson, you have been served."

There was a hardening of his eyes as he glanced from the envelope back to Martinez. His lips puckered with annoyance as he tossed the envelope over his shoulder without opening it.

Holding his ground and his gaze he said, "I really don't think you want a ticket for littering, just being released and all."

Pulling his bag from his shoulder he held it tightly to his side and replied, "You have my new address, I'm sure. Send me a bill."

Martinez placed his sunglasses back on his face and flicked his chin with his thumb before turning away.

Steve opened the passenger side back door to the Beamer, flung his bag onto the seat and turned back grinning mischievously as he stated, "Hey, be sure to tell Lizzy I said hello."

Opening the car door to his Impala, Martinez confidently said, "I'll be seeing you around, Robinson."

GIRLS' night on Fridays at Chip's was Elizabeth's favorite. She was able to get her Black Jack on and visit her friend Donny DeLuca in order to de-stress a little while China perused the horny rich men looking for a no-strings-attached kinda lady.

Chip's was banging like any other Friday night, especially during tourist season. After enjoying the amusement park for the day, many of the tourists and locals alike took their evening partying straight to the casino; not only for gambling but also for the live bands and dancing.

As the rest of the players waited impatiently for Elizabeth to make a decision, she was scanning the establishment. Donny gave her a concerned look. "Aye, doll, you okay," he asked.

Snapping out of her daze, she turned back to the table. "I'm so sorry." Glancing down at her cards, she held a four of spades and five of diamonds. She looked at the cards on the table and back to the dealer's hand. Donny currently held a two and his hole card. She nodded and smiled. "Hit me." The players to her left, stood where they were.

Donny flipped over his card, which was a jack of hearts. He dealt himself another. Ten of spades. Shaking his head in disappointment, he dished out the winnings to the players including Elizabeth.

Taking a deep breath she sighed.

Glancing up at her between dealing cards, Donny asked, "Yo, Liz, what's gotchu so down, doll? It's Friday and you're on a winning streak. Dat detective being good to ya?"

She loved the sound of his Jersey accent blended with the sympathy in his voice. Shaking off her anxiety and getting her head back in the game she replied, "I'm fine. Thanks, Donny. There's just a weird vibe tonight and I can't put my finger on it." Scanning her eyes across the room again, she waited to spot someone staring at her. *You're just being paranoid, Liz. Chill out.*

On the other side of the casino where the high rollers congregated, Danielle DuPont slid from her office and glided across the room in her sleek black, backless dress; her long red hair pulled into a bun and her bangs hanging slightly over her eyebrows to accentuate her green eyes. With Michelle Gardner awaiting trial for attempting to set up her husband, Richard, for hiring someone to kill her, Danielle officially took her place as the manager of the entire establishment.

She hammed it up with all the gentleman who were running exorbitant tabs as if they had nothing to lose and smiled flirtatiously through her red lips as they complimented her and asked her to forward their appreciations of the hospitality to Richard.

Being close to midnight, she walked up to one of the bars and asked the bartender for her usual glass of Chardonnay. As her drink was set down in front of her, she felt a presence in the seat next to her. A nicely built man sat down with his face turned away from her. "Oh, I'm so sorry, let me order you a drink?"

Steve turned towards her, his voice firm, and said, "By all means, Jenny..."

Although her demeanor remained placid, panic was rioting within her. Swallowing hard, she lifted her chin and boldly met his gaze.

"...Oh, wait. It's Danielle now, right? Been a long, long time since I've had the pleasure. Wouldn't you agree?"

FIND OUT WHAT HAPPENS IN, Strong Conviction!